A KILLER IN BLACK ROBES

"Mr. Slocum, this is my courtroom and these are my chambers. You will do as you are told in either room or I will find you in contempt and put you behind bars. Is that clear?"

Slocum shifted his weight.

His movement did not sit well with the judge, who reached into a desk drawer and pulled a pistol out. He set it on the table in front of him, the barrel pointed at Slocum, the judge's hand still on the butt of the little Smith & Wesson .38.

"I'm not going to shoot you, Judge," Slocum said.

"No, but if you don't sit down right this minute, I might shoot you where you stand and rule it self-defense."

Slocum hesitated.

The judge picked up the pistol again, aimed it at Slocum and cocked the hammer back.

The clicking sounded loud in the silence of the room.

The judge's finger curled around the trigger and his mouth stopped worrying the stub of cigar poking from between his grotesque little lips . . .

D0391882

JAKE LOGAN

SLOCUM

AND THE HANGMAN'S LADY

JOVE BOOKS, NEW YORK

THE BERKLEY PUBLISHING GROUP
Published by the Penguin Group
Penguin Group (USA) Inc.
375 Hudson Street, New York, New York 10014, USA
Penguin Group (Canada), 10 Alcorn Avenue, Toronto, Ontario M4V 3B2, Canada
(a division of Pearson Penguin Canada Inc.)
Penguin Books Ltd., 80 Strand, London WC2R 0RL, England
Penguin Group Ireland, 25 St. Stephen's Green, Dublin 2, Ireland (a division of Penguin Books Ltd.)
Penguin Group (Australia), 250 Camberwell Road, Camberwell, Victoria 3124, Australia
(a division of Pearson Australia Group Pty. Ltd.)
Penguin Books India Pvt. Ltd., 11 Community Centre, Panchsheel Park, New Delhi—110 017, India
Penguin Group (NZ), Cnr. Airborne and Rosedale Roads, Albany, Auckland 1310, New Zealand
(a division of Pearson New Zealand Ltd.)
Penguin Books (South Africa) (Pty.) Ltd., 24 Sturdee Avenue, Rosebank, Johannesburg 2196, South
Africa

Penguin Books Ltd., Registered Offices: 80 Strand, London WC2R 0RL, England

SLOCUM AND THE HANGMAN'S LADY

A Jove Book / published by arrangement with the author

PRINTING HISTORY
Jove edition / October 2004

ISBN: 0-515-13835-5

JOVE®
Jove an imprint The Berkley Publishing Group,
a division of Penguin Group (USA) Inc.
375 Hudson Street, New York, New York 10014.
JOVE is a registered trademark of Penguin Group (USA) Inc.
The "J" design is a trademark belonging to Penguin Group (USA) Inc.

PRINTED IN THE UNITED STATES OF AMERICA

10 9 8 7 6 5 4 3 2 1

1

John Slocum had never been so glad to get to a place as he was when he rode into Del Rio. It was hot and he was covered with dust, his rugged face scoured by wind and grit, his mouth as dry as the terrain he had just crossed.

He drew in the lead rope to keep the Arabian close to him and the black horse he rode, Ferro. He tightened his grip on the rope because people were staring at the beautiful Arabian he was leading, as well as at him and Ferro, an equally beautiful horse with a star blaze on its forehead. Ferro was a tough Morgan out of Tennessee, a distance horse with good bottom, strong legs, deep chest.

Just outside the village, Slocum saw a cemetery sitting atop a ridge. Some of the graves were adorned with bright, colorful flowers that fluttered like earthbound kites in the slight breeze. A few people walked among the crosses and headstones, or knelt before a mound of earth and stone, their hands pressed together in prayer.

The ridge rose to the top of a hill rocky and black, as barren as if a fire had swept over it, killing every living thing.

Just inside the town, Slocum saw a cart bearing a coffin

being pulled by a burro. A small cortege of mourners followed the *carreta*. The burnished bronze of their faces, their high cheekbones, told him that they were Mexicans. The women wore black and the men wore the white garb of peons, the breeze flapping the brims of their straw sombreros. Slocum touched a hand to the brim of his hat in a silent salute and one of the men, somber-faced, nodded in acknowledgment.

The cart creaked as he passed it and none of the women looked up at him. Their heads were bowed and some of them held rosary beads in their gnarled hands. One or two were weeping. He could almost feel the sadness in the air as Ferro picked up the pace.

Some of the people, Mexicans mostly, waved at Slocum as if he were some gringo messiah come to rescue them from poverty and the blazing heat of afternoon. Out of the corner of his eye, he caught a glimpse of an odd wooden structure near the plaza at the center of the city, but he paid no attention to it at the time. It stood in shadow, between a pair of adobe brick buildings and Ferro was into a trot by then at the smell of water. The town sat on the border between the United States and Mexico, separated only by the Rio Bravo, with its umber waters, its wavetops glinting silver in the sunlight as if sharp knives were rising and falling from its flowing surface.

He knew where to go. Hardesty had given him good directions. The livery stable was at the far end of town, overlooking the river, surrounded by little adobe dwellings with clay pots sprouting flowers in front of every door. A Mexican wearing a white shirt and trousers opened the gate to a small corral, one of many surrounding the livery, and Slocum rode in as if he had been expected, which he knew he was.

"You can cut him loose," a man said. Slocum looked

to the voice and saw a man emerge from the shadows of an overhanging roof that jutted from the livery barn.

Slocum reined up, pulled the dusky Arabian close, leaned over the saddle and slipped the halter from his face and neck. The horse bolted in a tight turn and began running around the fence, bobbing its head and flashing its dark brown tail in exultation at his sudden, but limited, freedom from the rope and halter.

"You can put your horse in here," the man said, his face shadowed by the brim of his Stetson. "He probably wants some grain and water."

The Mexican opened the gate for Slocum and he rode through. The gate closed behind him. He saw the Arabian stop at a trough and bow his head to drink. The man walked over to the fence nearest the horse and gazed at him in admiration. The Mexican at the gate grabbed Slocum's bridle and started walking toward the livery.

"Hold up," Slocum said. "I'll climb down."

The Mexican stopped and Slocum dismounted. As he did, he noticed men emerging from the shadows of the overhang. They carried rifles and shotguns and took up positions near the corral where the Arabian was quartered. Another Mexican emptied a tin of grain into a feed trough inside the corral, next to the fence. The stallion turned from the watering trough to the feed bin.

Slocum walked over to the man at the fence.

"Hardesty?" Slocum said.

"I'm Bill Hardesty. You must be Slocum." The man extended his hand. Slocum shook it and nodded.

"Why all the guards?" Slocum asked. "I mean that Arab stud is valuable, but . . ."

Hardesty laughed.

"The cost of the horse and your fee, Mr. Slocum, make him a very valuable animal, for sure. There are some here in Del Rio who would love to get their hands on such a fine stallion. I'm taking him to my ranch in the morning. But in the meantime, my caballeros will see that he stays put."

"Speaking of the cost . . ." Slocum said.

Hardesty smiled.

"If you don't mind, I'm going to invite you to supper tonight and I'll pay you then."

Slocum looked at the man. His handshake had been firm and his palm had not been sweaty. Hardesty had sky blue eyes and an open, honest face. If he owned a ranch, he looked to be a hands-on manager. His clothes were clean, but not new or showy. He didn't wear rings with diamonds or precious stones in them.

"I guess I can trust you, Mr. Hardesty."

"Call me Bill. And I'll call you John, if that's all right."

Slocum nodded.

"We'll eat at your hotel tonight, the best food in Del Rio. There are some people I want you to meet. I'll say this. You know your horses. You brought me exactly what I wanted."

"Well, you made it very clear what kind of horseflesh you were interested in. This is a young strong stud, a breeder. You can make money off of him."

"I know. He looks very sound. Does he have a name?"

"The man I bought him from called him Aladdin."

"Does a magic lamp come with him?"

"I asked the same question," Slocum said.

"And what did the man say?"

"He said that riding him was the magic lamp. The horse grants all wishes."

"Nicely said."

"Get your gear, John, and I'll take you to the Del Rio Hotel. I think Aladdin will be safe with my men guarding him."

Slocum sensed that there was more that Hardesty

wanted to say. Perhaps there was more to Del Rio than met the eye, an undercurrent of lawlessness that made Hardesty uncomfortable. "Well," Slocum thought, "I won't be here long. He'll pay me tonight and I can ride Ferro back to Missouri and buy more horses."

Slocum knew there'd be more business waiting for him in Kansas City. Good, well-bred horses sold for a premium out West.

He got his bedroll, saddlebags, rifle and the sawed-off shotgun wrapped in his blanket and followed Hardesty up the main street.

"One thing about Del Rio," Hardesty said. "You can walk to anyplace you want to go."

"Do you live in town?"

"Not me. My ranch lies about ten miles from here. I don't come into town much. Maybe once a month."

Again, Slocum sensed that there was a lot about Del Rio that Hardesty wasn't telling him. Maybe he'd loosen up that evening, over supper. Slocum was curious, but he wasn't going to press it. In the morning, he would be gone.

As Slocum and Hardesty came to the town square, which Slocum had passed without noticing, he saw an ominous sight off to the side. There was a platform on skids stuck between two buildings. There were, in fact, skid marks visible in the street where the wooden platform had been moved back fairly recently. In fact, people avoided that place. He saw footprints in the dust giving it a wide berth.

"That looks like a gallows," Slocum said.

"It is," Hardesty said. "There was a hanging here this morning."

"I've never seen a portable gallows."

"Well, that's the way the judge wanted it. It usually stays in an enclosure, but they haven't gotten around to moving it back inside yet. Maybe there'll be another hanging today. Or tomorrow."

Slocum's eyebrows arched.

"Most towns never have a hanging, and those that do maybe have only one a year or one every two or three years. Big cities, I mean."

Hardesty cleared his throat, as if he were embarrassed.

"They take crime seriously here in Del Rio," Hardesty said. "And the consequences are harsh."

"What do they do with horse thieves, Bill?"

"Oh, they hang them. Or shoot them first. Rustling, horse stealing are very serious crimes."

"Yes, I agree. I'm just surprised Del Rio has a permanent, portable gallows, that's all."

"It helps to remind people that crime doesn't pay."

It paid all right, Slocum thought. At least in Del Rio. It paid in death at the end of a rope.

2

Before he walked down the hotel stairs to the dining room, Slocum lit a cheroot, the first he'd smoked all day. But now he was in the evening cool, had bathed and brushed his clothes and black frock coat to rid them of the trail dust, cleaned his hat and shined his boots. He strapped on his gun belt, the holster with his double-action Colt .45, made sure his bellygun was tucked back behind his belt buckle, not showing, but within easy reach. He didn't expect trouble, but he was a stranger in a strange town, and it didn't hurt to be prepared for any eventuality.

He drew on the cheroot, released the smoke into the air. Now, he thought, the room was his own. It had his smell, his smoky stamp on it. He smiled at the humor of that thought and walked to the door. He stepped outside into the hall and closed the door. He was looking forward to a good meal, and some of the smells had wafted up the stairs, stirring the digestive juices in his stomach.

The dining room was crowded, humming with talk. Slocum stood at the entrance, gazing around, looking for Bill Hardesty. A thin pall of blue smoke hung suspended several feet above the tables as diners who had completed

their meals puffed on cigars and cigarettes. Slocum saw
a receptacle filled with sand and he drove his cheroot into
its center, snuffing it out.

A pretty woman approached him, coming from one of
the back tables. He had seen her weave her way through
the dining room out of the corner of his eye and now he
got a good look at her. He thought she was leaving, but
she strode straight up to him, stopped and looked him over
with bright blue eyes that sparkled with the shine of the
lamplight. He looked her over, too, dropping his gaze to
her small feet encased in expensive black patent leather
shoes with golden brass buckles, the long dress that clung
to her slender legs, the full breasts pressing invitingly
against her blue blouse. She had a symmetrical face with
prominent cheekbones, fair skin that was almost translu-
cent and a patrician nose with slightly flaring nostrils.
Luxuriant black hair that had the sheen of a crow's wing
in sunlight cascaded over her shoulders.

"Mr. Slocum," she said.

"Yes, ma'am." He took off his hat.

She laughed, and her mirth was a chromatic ripple up
and down the musical scale, like creek water burbling
over smooth shiny stones.

"I'm Lorelei," she said. "Lorelei Hardesty."

Slocum swallowed as a trace of her delicate perfume
washed over him like the scent of desert flowers in spring.

"Bill Hardesty's daughter."

"Oh, yes. He asked me to meet him here." Slocum
shifted his weight from one foot to the other and his fingers worried the brim of his hat. He felt as nervous as a
schoolboy.

"I'll take you to our table," she said, clasping his hand.
Her touch was warm and gentle as she guided him
through the maze of tables, to where Hardesty was sitting,
near the center of the large room. There was a bandstand

and the musicians were just stepping onto it. The elevated platform stood at the edge of a dance floor. As the musicians tuned up their instruments, Lorelei released his hand and ushered him to a chair next to her father's. Slocum pulled her chair out, the one flanking him, and she sat down. He moved the chair back and she gave him a glance of gratitude.

"Glad you could join us, John. I forgot to tell you that my daughter would be here."

"It was a pleasant surprise, Bill."

Lorelei smiled at him and Slocum smiled back.

Slocum sat down between Bill and Lorelei. Hardesty reached into an inside pocket of his coat and produced an envelope which he handed to Slocum.

"As agreed," he said.

Slocum slipped the envelope inside his coat.

"Thank you," he said.

"What will you have to drink, John?" Hardesty asked.

"Straight Kentucky whiskey."

"Ah, a man after my own heart, John." Hardesty signaled for a waiter. When one came over, Hardesty ordered two whiskies for himself and Slocum and a glass of Chardonnay for his daughter. When the drinks came, Hardesty ordered supper and the fare sounded good to Slocum.

"Hungry?" Hardesty asked.

"I could eat the southbound end of a northbound horse," Slocum said. "Begging your pardon, ma'am."

"Oh, you don't have to worry about Lorelei, John. She's heard it all."

"And said it all," she said.

Slocum laughed.

"John," she said. "May I call you John?"

"Sure," Slocum said.

"I want you to look at that table over there." She

crooked her neck to indicate where Slocum should look, without pointing with her finger.

Slocum looked in that direction.

"You might be interested in what's going on down here in our neck of the woods," she said. "That man in the dark suit is our local banker, Frank Rankins. He's very rich. Across the table from Frank—the man wearing the colorful shirt and the bolo tie—is a man named Norville Granby, Frank's client. The woman sitting next to Granby, wearing that beautiful gown, is his wife, Cordelia. They're from Colorado."

"Lorelei," Hardesty warned.

"Oh, Daddy, it's common knowledge."

Slocum had no idea what they were talking about. But he looked at Norville and his beautiful wife Cordelia. They did seem to stand out.

Lorelei went on, blithely ignoring her father's admonition.

"Granby is buying a hundred thousand acres of land next to our ranch," she said. "But apparently, he doesn't have all the money. So he's trying to arrange a short-term loan for the remainder from Mr. Rankins."

Slocum tasted the whiskey. It was warm in his throat. He wondered why Lorelei was telling him about these people. After tonight, he'd never see any of them again. He tried to look interested.

"He wants to move his cattle holdings down here from Colorado," Lorelei continued, "but he's run into a snag up in Colorado. He needs a six-month loan. He says the sale of his property up north ought to be completed well before that time."

"Lorelei," Hardesty said. "Why are you telling our guest all this? It's a private matter between the Granbys and Mr. Rankins."

"Because Cordelia saw the Arabian stallion John

brought down today and she said she and her husband need a man to wrangle their horses, some forty or fifty head that they want to bring down here. I just thought John might be interested."

Hardesty looked at Slocum.

"Well, John, are you? There's something mighty fishy about those Coloradoans."

"Daddy, whatever do you mean?" Lorelei said.

"Granby's buying a chunk of land right across from the Mexican border. It's almost useless for raising cattle. And it'll be costly to make it into good grazing land. He'll have a hell of a lot of fencing to do between that land and my spread. He'll need to plant hardy grass that would probably have to be imported from Africa, and while that's growing, his ten thousand head will be either starving to death or breaking down fences to graze on my land."

"Oh, Daddy, you're such a pessimist. You always look at the bad side of things."

"I try to look at the practical side. I wonder if Rankins knows what he's buying into."

Slocum noticed a man sitting alone at a table. The man kept looking at the entrance to the dining room as if he were expecting someone. Like the Granbys, he didn't seem to fit in with the crowd in the hotel. He stood out like a sore thumb with his ill-fitting new suit. He wore a bandanna around his neck as if he were expecting a sandstorm to blow through the room at any moment. His long hair drooped down the back in a single braid that reached nearly to his waist. His skin was the color of tea, dark tea, so that Slocum thought he might be a half-breed, part Indian, but not Mexican. Slocum could not tell if he was armed, since he wore a waistcoat, which was the color of cream. He had no food in front of him and seemed to be nursing a cup of coffee. Slocum could see the steam rise when the man brought the cup to his lips.

Slocum forgot about the lone man when the waiter served their food. He looked down at his plate. Like the others, it was covered with hot *carne asada, papas fritas, frijoles rojos*, seasoned beefsteak cut into thin strips, fried potatoes and red beans. Slocum finished his whiskey and put a napkin on his lap. Hardesty made small talk during the meal and then ordered coffee and brandy.

While they were waiting for their drinks, Slocum offered Hardesty a cheroot. Hardesty took it. Slocum put one in his mouth and saw Hardesty fish out a matchbox and strike one on the sandpaper side.

"Aren't you going to offer me one, John?" Lorelei asked.

"Lorelei," Hardesty snapped, a frown on his face.

"I'd like to try one," she said.

Slocum reached into his pocket and slipped out another cigar. He was getting low; he'd have to buy more before he left town. And a bottle of whiskey, too, while he was at it.

Hardesty lit their cheroots. Slocum leaned back and looked at the man sitting by himself again. The man was still staring at the entrance, as if waiting for someone.

Then, a woman, very well dressed in a tight-fitting dark dress with lace above the bodice, swept into the room and walked over to the man's table. A veil softly obscured her face. Without a word, she held out her hand. He took it and stood up.

The band was playing a slow reel and the couple joined others on the dance floor.

The waiter brought the coffee and brandy.

Slocum was about to lift the snifter to his lips when he saw the couple glide by the banker's table. His jaw dropped when he saw the woman pull out a small pistol and squeeze the trigger.

A loud explosion boomed through the dining room. The pistol belched fire and a billowing cloud of white smoke. The patrons all turned their heads and the music stopped.

Then, pandemonium broke out. Several women screamed.

Slocum reached for the Colt on his hip.

Before he could draw his pistol, he felt a hand grasp his wrist and tighten around it.

For a moment, Slocum thought that he might be the next to die.

3

Slocum had seen Norville Granby take the bullet straight in his heart. The rancher now slumped in his chair, stone dead. It seemed to Slocum like he was watching everything in slow motion. He had seen the woman, still in the odd young man's arms, swirl on the dance floor straight over to the banker's table. He had seen her stretch out a hand with a small pistol in it and fire at point-blank range.

Slocum had gone for his gun when the veiled woman had raised her hand again, her pistol pointed straight at him. But to his surprise, instead of firing the woman had turned quickly and shoved the pistol into the hand of the man she had been dancing with seconds before. Then, in the confusion, Slocum had seen her run from the dining room and disappear.

"No gunplay," Slocum heard Hardesty's voice.

Slocum turned and looked Hardesty in the eyes. Then he saw that it was the rancher's hand that was gripping his wrist.

"No need, now, Bill. Just let go of my wrist," Slocum said.

Hardesty did as he was told.

"Don't ever do that again, Hardesty," Slocum said.

"I thought you were going to mix us into that."

"Did you see the shooting?"

"No, I was watching you."

"Well, next time, you'd better make sure you know where to look."

Before Hardesty could say anything, the room was filled with constables and sheriff's deputies. They swarmed around the ruddy-faced man who was still holding the smoking pistol.

Slocum got up from the table, pushing away his chair and walked over to where Granby was still slumped over, a hole in his chest right over his heart. There was very little blood, since his heart had stopped pumping right away. Hardesty came up and stood behind Slocum.

Granby's eyes were open. He was staring into eternity, the chill frost of death clouding his sightless eyes. Two deputies wrestled the hapless man with the braided hair, while another snatched the pistol from his hand.

"You're making a mistake," Slocum said.

"Mister, stay out of it, or I'll put you in the *cárcel*, along with this murderer."

"But he didn't shoot that man," Slocum said. "I saw who did it."

"We got witnesses who say he did."

"This man was dancing with a woman. She shot that banker."

The deputy's face hardened into a scowl. He looked at his prisoner.

"Was you dancin' with a woman?"

The man didn't answer. The deputy slapped him across the face with the back of his hand.

"You answer me, mister."

The man shook his head. The deputy raised his hand to strike the prisoner again.

"Deputy," Slocum said, "if you hit that man again, you'll be on the floor next to that dead rancher."

The deputy glared at Slocum. But he lowered his hand.

"Take him away," the deputy growled. "Lock him up."

The deputy walked around the table and confronted Slocum.

"And just who are you?" he asked.

Slocum told him.

"He's with me," Hardesty said. "He had nothing to do with any of this."

The deputy looked at Hardesty.

"Oh, hello, Mr. Hardesty. Didn't see you. If you said he had nothing to do with this killin', then you make sure he keeps his mouth shut. Mr. Granby had some friends in this town and we got a clear case here. Judge Wyman won't have no trouble convictin' that breed."

"Thanks, Smitty," Hardesty said. "Mr. Slocum and I will let you do your job."

"What's your name?" Slocum asked. "Smith?"

"Deputy Harold Smith to you, Slocum."

"Well, Deputy Smith, I saw the whole thing. That man you took to jail was dancing with a woman. She pulled out a pistol when she was close to Mr. Granby and shot him in the heart. Then she shoved the pistol into your prisoner's hand and ran out of the dining room."

"So you say."

"So I say," Slocum said.

"Well, you can tell it to the judge, Slocum."

With that, Smitty turned on his heel and left to talk to the other constables and deputies. They lifted Granby from the chair after determining that he was stone dead and carried him into the hotel lobby. Soon, the room began to clear. Hardesty and Slocum joined Lorelei back at their table.

They sat down. Lorelei was visibly shaken over the murder of Granby. Her hands were trembling and her lower lip quivered.

"Oh, Daddy," she said. "This is all so horrible."

"Yes, Lorelei. But the sheriff has the murderer. He'll go before Judge Wyman in the morning and probably be hanged before noon."

"What?" Slocum was aghast.

"Justice is swift in Del Rio."

"You mean railroading, don't you?" Slocum's anger was building by the moment.

"Judge Wyman will hear the evidence. He's fair."

"Well, I have evidence," Slocum said.

"And the judge will weigh it, John, I assure you."

They sat there as the dining room began to empty even more. They drank their brandies and smoked their cheroots. Slocum wore a thoughtful look on his face, his forehead creasing, his eyes squinting to narrow slits.

What he had seen here tonight was very mysterious, to say the least. Mysterious and puzzling. None of it made any sense to him just then, and he supposed it was because he did not know any of the people involved. Why would a woman murder a man in a public place? There had to be some underlying reason that Slocum couldn't fathom with the sparse information he had. Why would the lone man let himself be set up like that? Did he know the woman? Was she the one he had been waiting for, and if so, why? It was obvious to Slocum that the two came from different stations in life. He had the look of a working cowhand or farm laborer. She had an elegance about her, the way she dressed, the way she danced. She seemed at home in such a fancy dining hall, and the man seemed out of place.

"John," Hardesty said, "there's nothing you can do tonight. Sleep on it. If you still feel the way you do, you can go to court in the morning. It opens at nine o'clock."

"I wanted to go to the jail and talk to the prisoner," Slocum said.

"Why?"

"Curiosity. There's something out of place here, Bill. It looks to me like that man was deliberately framed. What connection does he have to Granby? Have you or Lorelei ever seen him before?"

Hardesty and his daughter both shook their heads.

"How about the woman? Did she look familiar to either of you?"

"I didn't notice her that much," Hardesty said. "I mean I saw a woman out of the corner of my eye, leaving the room. She didn't seem to be running. She just walked through the crowd, didn't she?"

"Yes," Slocum said. "She walked fast and deliberate. But she wasn't running. Did you get a good look at her, Lorelei?"

"I saw her dancing with that man, but I didn't pay much attention," she said. "She was well-dressed, and I remember wondering why she wore a veil. I thought she might be a woman in mourning. It was only a fleeting glance, though, just before Mr. Granby was shot."

"Did you see her shoot him?" Slocum asked. "Either of you?"

"I'm sorry, John," Hardesty said. "I just heard the gunshot."

"Me, too," Lorelei said.

"Do you have any idea who the woman might be? Do you know anyone who wears a veil in public?"

"No," Lorelei said. "Unless a woman's in mourning. And that's very rare around here."

Slocum looked at Hardesty, who shook his head.

"Look, John, if it'll make you feel any better, I'll go over to the jail and see if I can find out who the man was that they locked up."

"Ever see him before? Either of you?"

Both Lorelei and her father shook their heads.

"No, never mind," Slocum said. "I'll go over there in the morning. Courthouse near the jail?"

"Right next to it," Hardesty said. "I'll go with you. Lorelei, you'd better turn in. I've got some things to do at the stables and I'll be up in a while."

Lorelei nodded.

"I'm going to turn in, too," Slocum said.

"Good, you can escort me, then," Lorelei said. "My room's right next to yours."

"I'll see you in the morning, Sugar," Hardesty said to his daughter. "Good night, John."

"Good night, Bill. Thanks for the supper."

"My pleasure."

Hardesty walked to the counter and paid the bill as Lorelei and Slocum entered the hotel lobby. They walked up the stairs together. She walked very close to him and her hip brushed against his leg several times on the way up the stairs.

At Lorelei's door, Slocum stood there politely as she inserted the key.

"Won't you come in, John? I've some brandy in my room."

"But your father . . ."

"Oh, his room's on another floor. I thought we might talk and look out my window at the night. It's such a lovely cool evening. I have a balcony."

"I'm not much on brandy, Lorelei."

"Whiskey, then. Straight Kentucky bourbon, is it?"

"Yes," he said, his voice full of husk.

"Besides, I'd like another cheroot, if you can spare one?"

"Sure," he said.

She opened the door, walked to a table and struck a match. She lit the oil lamp, which threw a golden cone along the wall, revealing the outlines of comfortable furniture. Slocum followed her in and closed the door.

He swallowed hard.

Lorelei was slipping out of her dress. She let it fall to the floor in a puddle.

She had nothing on underneath.

4

Lorelei was all woman.

She stood there by the lighted lamp, statuesque, cool and elegant, letting Slocum drink in her natural beauty. She smiled. Slocum tried to smile back, but his face was frozen in rigid surprise. He hadn't expected this. Lorelei had given no indication during supper that she was a willing woman.

"Come," she said. "I'll show you the way to my bed. Don't you have to work up an appetite for whiskey? Especially after a full meal?"

"Yeah, I reckon," Slocum croaked.

The bed was in a far section of the room, against a wall with no window. There was a table next to it and at the foot of the bed another table. She pointed to it as she sat down and crossed her elegant legs.

"You can put your clothes there, John," she said. Then she touched a post near the head of the bed. "You can hang your pistol here, if it will make you more comfortable."

"I'm not a gunman," he said.

"No, but you wear one. And I have the feeling you know how to use it."

Slocum said nothing. He undressed and hung his pistol on the bedpost, within easy reach. When he peeled off his shirt, Lorelei's eyes widened.

"My," she said, "you even have a hideout gun."

Slocum looked down, pulled the Remington bellygun from inside his belt.

"It comes in handy sometimes," he said, laying it on the side table. He didn't expect to have to use it on Lorelei or anyone else, for that matter.

He took off his stovepipe boots with the bowie knife concealed in one of them. He was glad Lorelei couldn't see it. He didn't want to give her the wrong impression. But the knife, too, came in handy sometimes. Most fights with other men happened up close, and the kind of men he had to fight seldom, if ever, played fair. An ace in the hole, or two, could often mean the difference between life and death.

He slid into bed beside her as she scooted over and lay on her back, an enigmatic smile on her lips.

"Why?" he asked, his voice just above a whisper.

"Why this? Inviting you to my bed?"

"Yes."

"Del Rio is short on real men, John. A girl can knit or sew, make quilts, or peel potatoes. And she can throw plates at the wall, or cry herself to sleep every night. Many of our women do just that. And that's all they do. I took one look at you and put down my needle and thread. I'd rather make love."

"A girl after my own heart."

He leaned over and kissed her. Her body shivered as if he had sent a shot of static electricity through her body.

"Umm," she said. "You know how to kiss, John. It's been a long time since I felt like this, all warm inside, my stomach fluttering as if it were full of butterflies. Can you do more than that?"

She looked at him, pooching out her lips for another kiss. He leaned over and she put her arms around him, drew him down to her so that his chest was crushing one of her breasts. The left one.

Lorelei purred like a kitten.

He mounted her then, as she spread her legs to receive him. He slid into her steamy sheath, feeling the warmth of her suffuse his flesh. She cooed with delight as he sank deep into the velvety folds of her sex. She arched her back and grabbed his hips with both hands, pulling at him as he rose and fell in a slow, steady rhythm that gradually increased in intensity.

"It's good, John," she breathed.

"Yes, Lorelei. Very good."

"You're the answer to a lonesome gal's prayers."

She lunged at him with her hips, impaling him, her hands gripping his hips hard, holding him as she thrashed wildly, the bed creaking under their weight, groaning with their vigorous movements.

"Never, never so good," she sighed as she bucked beneath him, her fingernails digging into his flesh, her legs rising up and down with his every thrust.

Slocum saw her skin flush from excitement, turning from an almost alabaster whiteness to a rosy burn as if she had lain in the sun too long. The color spread up from her breasts to her throat until it turned a raspberry hue. She rose and fell with him in an undulating rhythm as their passions mingled and grew in force.

Her eyelashes fluttered, her lids opening and closing, as if she were drifting in and out of a state of sheer ecstasy. Her mouth opened and her lips quivered as she breathed little sighs of pleasure with each powerful thrust.

His cock throbbed and swelled with engorged blood as his own excitement rose to match Lorelei's. He immersed himself in her steamy depths until she convulsed with an electric shock. Her body quivered against his own until his veins sang with the floodtide of his rushing blood, his heart pumping fast like a man racing against the wind.

With powerful thrusts, Slocum took Lorelei to the heights of ecstasy. She thrashed and moaned with pleasure, holding on to him like a woman afraid of falling from a high cliff. He plumbed her depths with his prick, sliding in and out until her rapture erupted in soft screams.

"Umm, so good," she panted. "I'm flying like a bird."

"You're some woman, Lorelei," Slocum said, marveling at her energy, the power in her loins.

The muscles of her cunt closed tight around his cock as she clamped her legs against his hips. She shuddered with still another orgasm and put a hand over her mouth to keep from screaming. Slocum grabbed her by the waist and pulled her hips upward as he drove even deeper into her. This time she screamed softly as still another climax rippled through her body. Sweat sheened her skin and she wriggled beneath him, gazing up into his blue eyes, stroking his long black hair.

"Go there with me, John," she purred. "Go up to the top with me and fill me with your seed."

They had been at it for a good fifteen minutes and Slocum wanted to make sure that she was fully satisfied.

"I can wait," he said.

"I don't want you to wait any longer. I want you to be satisfied, as I am."

"It will be a quick ride," he said.

"The quicker the better."

He increased his tempo, gradually, so that she could build to still another climax. He slid in and out of her with a practiced slowness, letting her feel every inch of him. She rocked with him, then, exulting in the hard sure strokes that penetrated the folds of her cunt, making every nerve end tingle as if charged with electricity. Faster and faster, Slocum plumbed her and then her eyes glazed over and her mouth went slack. He could feel her rising up beneath him, hanging on to him, anticipating the climax that was to come in a few seconds.

Then, with blinding speed, he took her over the top and rose up with her, racing to the summit of the highest peak. She screamed in his ear and his balls exploded, spewing his milk into her cup. She moaned with pleasure and her loins quivered in the final throes of a resounding climax. Slocum collapsed atop her glistening body and buried his face in her damp hair.

"Oh, John," she sighed. "Oh, John."

She hugged him fiercely for a long moment as he went limp inside her. They lay there, floating gently back to earth like two downy feathers. The room filled with silence, punctuated only by their breathing.

She moved and spewed him out and he lay by her side on his back.

"Thank you, John," she breathed, her hand resting on his belly. "I haven't felt so much like a woman as I do at this moment. You've restored something in me that I thought I had lost."

"You don't lose what you have, Lorelei."

She laughed.

"And you say the right things, too."

"So do you," he said.

"I've been trying to figure out your accent. It's faint, but it's not Texan. And it's not Missouri either."

"It's Calhoun County, Georgia," he said. "What's left of it."

"Your voice is very deep and soft and yes, now I can hear Georgia in it. And you're a gentleman, too. A gentle man."

"Why thank you, Miss Lorelei," he said, exaggerating

his southern accent straight out of Georgia. "And I like your Texas twang, too."

They both laughed.

"Would you like some of that brandy now?" she asked.

"I'd rather have whiskey," he said.

"Then, you shall have it," she said, gliding from the bed and onto her feet. She walked to a wooden cabinet and opened the doors, revealing bottles that glistened in the light from the lamp. She bent down and he heard the tinkling of glass. She pulled out a bottle of Old Taylor.

"Is this all right, John?"

"Of course."

He slid from the bed and stood up, his muscles rippling under the sheen of sweat that covered his body.

Lorelei poured Slocum a generous glass of whiskey. As he drank, she looked at him, her gaze roving over him with a look of admiration on her face.

"How's the taste?" she asked, pouring herself a snifter of brandy.

"Smooth," he said.

"Just like you, John."

He laughed.

They clinked glasses and took sips from their drinks.

"Let's sit down on the divan," Lorelei said. "We'll be more comfortable there."

"Suits me," Slocum said.

As they were walking toward the divan, they both heard a commotion next door.

"What's that?" she asked.

Slocum heard a rattling sound, then a dull thud.

"It sounds like it's coming from your room, John."

A moment later, Slocum heard another loud crash, then a splintering of wood. And it did sound as if it were coming from his room, right next door.

Lorelei, frightened, her face suddenly pale, with worry

lines etching her forehead, moved close to Slocum, as if
for protection.

Slocum froze as they both heard the loud explosion
from a gunshot. Then two more shots boomed out and he
distinctly heard the spatter of buckshot striking wood.

Lorelei screamed as more shots rang out.

And then they both heard pounding footsteps out in the
hall, as if two or more people were running away, down
the corridor.

Then, it was silent and Slocum realized that Lorelei
was clutching his arm as if hanging desperately onto a life
raft in the middle of a storm-tossed ocean.

5

Slocum sprang into action, dressing quickly, strapping on his gun belt as the tang of gunpowder assailed his nostrils. Lorelei hurriedly donned a dress she snatched from the wardrobe, but Slocum was already out the door and into the hall, his pistol drawn. He moved in a crouch to the door of his room, ready to shoot if threatened.

The door to Slocum's room had been kicked in so that it hung askew on bent hinges, agape, leaning inside the room. Wisps of white smoke still hung in the air and the smell of gunpowder stung Slocum's nostrils. Cautiously, he stepped inside, gun drawn, still in a fighting crouch.

Feathers from the pillows on his bed still floated in the air or clung to the drapes and lay scattered on the floor like tufts of cotton. The bed was riddled with buckshot and so were the walls. The glass panes in the windows were shattered and shards of glass lay below the sills. From his observation, Slocum guessed that whoever had broken into his room had blasted every part of it with a double-barreled shotgun. Luckily, his bedroll, rifle and shotgun, all lay under the bed on the far side, away from the door, so that they were untouched by shotgun pellets.

He reached down and picked one up just as Lorelei came into the room. A loud gasp escaped her lips.

"Double ought buck," Slocum said.

"They—they meant to kill you," she said.

"If I had been anywhere in this room, I would have been shot up, that's for sure."

Lorelei gasped again. She glanced around the room with eyes wide open in a look of amazement.

"It's just awful," she said. "Who could have done such a thing?"

"That's what I'd like to know."

They both heard footsteps coming up the stairs, and then the sound of someone running down the hall toward Slocum's room. They heard footsteps coming from the floor above them as well.

Two men entered the room with guns drawn. Slocum cocked his pistol.

"Just hold it right there," Slocum said.

"I'm the sheriff," one of the men said. He pointed to a star on his chest.

"And, I'm his deputy," the other man said, opening his vest to reveal a similar star pinned to his shirt.

"Maybe if we all holster our guns," Slocum said, "we can talk. First of all, tell me your names and I'll tell you mine."

The two men hesitated, then slid their pistols back in their holsters. Slocum eased the hammer back down on his Colt and slipped his pistol back in its sheath.

"I know who you are, Slocum," the sheriff said. "I'm Blandings, Curtis Blandings, sheriff of Del Rio."

Slocum turned his head to look at the deputy.

"Uh, I'm Larry Jones, Mr. Blandings's deputy."

More footsteps pounded down the hall. Lorelei's father stood framed in the doorway, a look of concern on his face.

"Come on in, Mr. Hardesty," Blandings said. "Maybe we can get to the bottom of this. What happened, Slocum?"

"Take a look, Sheriff. Someone broke into my room and opened up with shotguns and pistols."

Blandings and Jones scanned the room. Jones's mouth opened and his jaw dropped. Blandings's eyes narrowed to twin slits.

"Golly," Jones said.

"Missed you, eh, Slocum? All that flying lead," Blandings said. "How did that happen?"

"He wasn't here," Lorelei said. Slocum looked at her in surprise.

Blandings's eyebrows arched in surprise. Then, a rosy flush spread across his face.

Lorelei smiled knowingly. "He was next door," she said. "With me. In my room."

"Yes'm," Blandings said. He looked to his deputy. "Larry, get a whiff of Slocum's pistol. You don't mind, Slocum?"

Slocum pulled his pistol from its holster, held it as Jones walked over and sniffed the barrel.

"It ain't been shot," Jones said. He stepped away. Slocum reholstered the Colt.

"Maybe you can tell me how you know my name, Sheriff," Slocum said.

"I heard you got a big mouth, Slocum. We arrested a man for murder tonight and you want to piss in the pickle barrel."

"That man you arrested didn't kill anybody, Blandings. You've got the wrong man."

"That's up to the judge. We got witnesses say he killed Granby. In cold blood."

"A woman shot Granby. Then she tossed the pistol to that man you arrested."

"So you say. Want some advice, Slocum?"

"Not particularly."

"If you want to stay alive, and out of trouble, you'll get on your horse and ride out of Del Rio at first light."

"And let an innocent man hang?" Slocum said.

The sheriff shrugged.

"It's your call. It might boil down to your life or his."

"Blandings, I don't know what your sense of justice is, but to me it means a hell of a lot. The Mexicans have a saying: *'No hay justicia en el mundo.'* 'There is no justice in the world.' And, they're right. As long as men turn their backs on justice, there just won't be any."

"You got mighty high ideals, Slocum. And that may be commendable in some circumstances. But we have justice in Del Rio, same as any place else. And we got us a judge who dispenses it without never blinking an eye."

"Hanging an innocent man is not justice," Slocum persisted.

He felt a tug on his arm and turned to see Lorelei standing next to him. Silently, she was asking him to back away, leave the argument. In this case, he thought she might be right. He would get nowhere with this sheriff, or his deputy. They were as blind as bats, and like some lawmen he had seen, they took the easy path. None of them liked open cases. When they had a good suspect and enough evidence to convict, they closed their eyes to any other possibilities. It seemed to Slocum that the judge in Del Rio was going to hang the man they had in custody, whether he was guilty or not.

"Slocum," Blandings said. "My advice still stands. Ride out in the morning and forget how close you came to getting killed tonight. You'll sleep a whole lot better once you get back to wherever it is that you live."

"I'll think about it, Blandings," Slocum said, fishing in

his coat pocket for a cheroot. "Meanwhile, I want a refund on my room."

"I'll see to it," Blandings said. "Bill? Can you put Slocum up in your room?" He turned to Hardesty.

"I'm sure we can work it out, Curtis."

"All right. You all clear out. I want to give this place a combing, see if we can find evidence of who wanted to put Slocum's lamp out."

Slocum walked to the other side of the bed and retrieved his bedroll with the double-barreled Greener wrapped inside, along with his '74 Winchester and its scabbard.

The sheriff looked at the articles in Slocum's hands with suspicion.

"You won't smell any burnt powder on my rifle, either, Blandings," Slocum said.

The sheriff threw up a hand in surrender.

"Go," Blandings said.

Lorelei took Slocum's arm and joined her father. The three of them left the room and walked back to Lorelei's quarters.

Inside Lorelei's room, Hardesty sat on the divan, next to his daughter. Slocum set his gear down and sat on a chair next to a small table. He took off his hat when Hardesty removed his.

"Well, John," Hardesty said, "are you going to take Curtis Blandings's advice and leave town in the morning?"

"Do you want me to?"

"I think it would be best."

"Why?"

Hardesty took in a breath and sank back on the divan. Lorelei stared at her father, a surprised look on her face.

"Look what you've stirred up. Somebody tried to kill you. They might try again."

"I've considered that," Slocum said.

"And?"

"First, let me ask you a question that's been nagging me, Bill."

"Go ahead."

"The woman who shot that rancher, Granby. It was a deliberate act. Did it have any connection to the sale of that land to Granby?"

"How would I know?"

Slocum leaned forward in his chair, staring directly into Hardesty's eyes.

"What happens to the land sale now? You'd know that, wouldn't you?"

Hardesty squirmed.

"I, uh, I suppose Mrs. Granby will have to borrow the money if she still wants the land."

"Mr. Granby was pretty anxious to get that land, wasn't he?"

"John, what are you driving at?" Lorelei asked.

"Your father knows, I think."

Lorelei reared up in shock, her back straight, her eyes flashing.

Hardesty patted the back of his daughter's hand to soothe her, calm her down.

"It's all right, Lorelei. It's not a secret exactly. John, that's a pretty valuable chunk of land, lying along the river as it does. I admit I wanted to buy it and was hoping that the deal with Granby would fall through. But, I didn't have anything to do with Norville Granby's death. Rankins has turned me down for a loan before. There's no reason to believe he's changed his mind about lending money for that land."

"What's Norville's wife's name?" Slocum asked.

"Cordelia," Lorelei said, still miffed that Slocum was grilling her father.

"Will Rankins go ahead and grant her the loan?" Slocum asked.

Hardesty shook his head.

"I don't know," he said. "Why?"

"Because," Slocum said, "if Rankins will loan her the money for that land, then Granby's wife is in danger."

Lorelei's face went white as all the color drained from it.

Hardesty scowled and cleared his throat.

Slocum stared at the rancher, wondering what was going on in his mind.

One thing was sure, Slocum thought, Hardesty wasn't telling him all that he knew about Granby's murder. The man was holding back and guarding a damned big secret.

Slocum meant to find out what that secret was if it was the last thing he ever did.

6

When Slocum went to the jail the next morning, he was told that he could not visit the prisoner held there for murder. Nor would they give Slocum the name of the man they were holding in a cell.

"You can see him in court," the jailer said. "Court's at nine o'clock. Hanging's at noon."

Slocum felt a cold chill run up and down his spine.

"So, that's the way it is," Slocum said.

"That's the way it is, mister."

The courtroom was not crowded. It was crudely furnished, except for the imposing judge's bench, which loomed over the seats that looked as if they had once been pews in an old southern church. They had been sanded and polished and painted, but he could tell that the wood was old and had been weathered before being placed in the Del Rio courtroom.

Slocum sat down and watched as the bailiff came in and out, placing papers on the judge's raised cherry wood desk. Attorneys, dressed in morning coats and ties, came and went, spoke in whispers at their respective counselors' tables. A young woman, pretty, dark-skinned, dark-eyed, dark-haired, came in and sat down near Slocum in one of the back rows. She wore a black lace shawl and a red and blue blouse tucked into an equally colorful skirt. She looked Indian or mestiza, perhaps Mexican, or perhaps part Spanish.

Slocum was early, but he didn't want to miss a chance to speak up on behalf of the accused. The large Waterbury clock on the wall indicated he had another fifteen minutes to wait for court to be in session. That is, if the judge was on time. The judge's name was Andrew J. Wyman, as the wooden sign on his bench indicated in bright brass lettering.

The dusky woman kept stealing glances at Slocum. And every time he turned to look at her, she turned her head away, as if afraid of being caught gazing at him. Finally, she did not turn away and Slocum gave her a reassuring smile. She got up from her pew and made her way over to where Slocum sat. She sat down next to him, wringing her hands as if she were trying to find the words she wanted to say to him.

"I'm John Slocum," he said.

"And you're here to see the judge sentence a man to death."

"I'm here to try and stop him from hanging an innocent man. And you?"

"Oh, Mr. Slocum. You are the one. I was hoping you were."

"The one?"

"The man who told the sheriff that my brother did not kill that man last night."

"The prisoner on trial is your brother?" Slocum's face registered surprise.

"Yes. His name is Luis Delgado. I am Carmen Delgado. We are from a poor family here in Del Rio. Luis is a dancer. We are both dancers. We dance for money. Our American mother taught us."

"Why was your brother at the Hotel Del Rio last night dancing with a woman? The woman who shot that man in cold blood."

"Ah, that is what I do not know. Except that he was paid to dance at the hotel. He did not know why."

"Tell me what happened, Carmen. Before your brother went to the hotel."

"My brother and I were dancing at a small fiesta in the barrio Hidalgo, a small community to the east of town. A man and a woman drove up in a buggy pulled by one horse. The woman, she wore a veil and we thought she was in mourning. The man, the one who drove the horse pulling the buggy, got out and spoke to my brother. He say, my brother told me, that the woman wishes to speak to him. My brother, he go over to the buggy and the woman give him some money. She say she wish to dance with him and tell him to meet her at the hotel last night. She say she will pay him much more money if my brother he do this."

"Do you know who the woman was?" Slocum asked.

Carmen shook her head.

"I do not know who she is. I could not see her face. My brother, he do not know either, I think."

"What about the driver? Do you know who he was?"

"I know what he looks like. I do not know him. But he is here. In the court."

"What? He's here? Now?"

"I see him come into the court with the papers. Oh, there he is again."

Carmen did not point, but she cocked her head to one side in the direction where she saw the man. Just entering the courtroom again was the bailiff. He was carrying more papers. He wore a badge and a pistol. He was a big, florid-faced man, wearing a fairly new Stetson hat. He had orange sideburns that matched his hair, a shock of reddish hair that was straight and spiked, stuck out on both sides of his hat.

"The bailiff was the man who drove the woman out to see your brother?"

"Yes. He is the one."

Slocum studied the bailiff, surprised at Carmen's revelation. What was the connection between the bailiff and the lady who murdered Granby? Who was she? And why did she set up an innocent man? What kind of heartless woman could do such a thing? Slocum knew there was a lot more to the case than he had first thought.

"Do you know the bailiff's name?" Slocum asked Carmen.

"No," she said.

Slocum knew he could find that out easily enough. He would still have to trace out all the connections. By rights, he knew he should have taken the sheriff's advice and be riding well away from Del Rio by now. But he couldn't stand the thought of seeing an innocent man hanged for something he didn't do. The injustice of it galled him and he could not live with his conscience if he didn't at least try to do something about it.

He knew what injustice was, Slocum did, and he knew what it was like for an innocent man to die. During the war, he had ridden for a time with Quantrill and his Raiders. When Quantrill hit Lawrence, Kansas, some of the men under his leadership went wild. They began shooting and raping and burning. But one incident stood out and he had never been able to erase the memory of it from his mind.

Some men were holed up in a house with women and children. Quantrill's men rode up and demanded that the men come out and surrender, assuring them that they would not be harmed. The women and children came outside and stood on the porch. The trooper in charge of the patrol told the women that their husbands would not be hurt. He told the children that they would not take their fathers away from them. All they wanted, they said, was for the men to come out and surrender. They would be treated kindly and be allowed to return to their families after Quantrill left Lawrence.

The men inside the house believed the man who spoke to their wives. The wives and children begged their husbands and fathers to come outside and surrender to the nice men on horseback. Even Slocum believed that the soldiers would show mercy.

Instead, the men came out, hugged their wives, kissed them, then walked off the porch toward the soldiers, their hands over their heads, and all hell broke loose. Quantrill's men opened fire and shot the men to rags in front of their wives and children. The soldiers laughed and rode away, leaving the bleeding men to die in front of their home, cradled in the arms of their women.

Slocum got sick and rode away from Lawrence and Quantrill, never to return. Later, he tracked down the four men who had committed the massacre, found them in St. Joe, Missouri, and called them out. He showed them the same mercy that they showed the innocent civilians they slaughtered in Lawrence.

Slocum looked up at the clock on the wall. The hands stood at five minutes until nine.

Then the bailiff opened a gate in the railing that separated the spectators from the counsel tables and headed toward them along the hardwood center aisle. He stopped and looked at Carmen and Slocum.

"Are you witnesses for any of the cases being heard this morning?"

"I am," Carmen said.

"What about you? You're Slocum, ain't ye?"

"I am. I'm here as a witness, too."

"Ma'am, you wait outside the courtroom. There are benches in the hall. Slocum, you come with me. Judge Wyman wants to talk to you."

Carmen shot Slocum a look, as if she suspected him of betraying her. Slocum shook his head, held out his hands and shrugged.

Slocum followed the bailiff back down the aisle as Carmen left the courtroom. The two men passed through the gate and the door the bailiff had been using to enter and leave the courtroom.

Then Slocum followed the bailiff down a hallway to a room with the judge's name on it. The bailiff knocked, then opened the door.

Judge Wyman sat behind a large desk in front of a window. He looked, Slocum thought, like a gargoyle guarding the entrance to a government building lined with columns. His eyes bulged from a paunchy face with bulldog folds of skin marring his countenance. He had a small mouth with flabby lips that glistened with saliva. He chewed on a fat cigar. His black robe looked freshly pressed. His bald pate jutted out from it like an obscene bust of a living head sitting atop a draped display table.

"This is Slocum," the bailiff said.

"Thank you, Rufus. You may go. Wait outside my door."

"Yes, sir, Judge."

Slocum stood there as the judge eyed him with those large fish eyes.

"You come armed to my courtroom, sir?" Wyman said.

"I didn't see any signs outside."

"Well, sit down."

"I'll stand."

"Sir, if you don't sit down, I'll call Mr. Early back in

here and have him take you to jail for contempt."

"Is this how you treat witnesses?" Slocum asked.

"First of all, Mr. Slocum, I determine who the witnesses will be, not you. And secondly, this is my courtroom and these are my chambers. You will do as you are told in either room or I will find you in contempt and put you behind bars. Is that clear?"

Slocum shifted his weight.

His movement did not sit well with the judge, who reached into a desk drawer and pulled a pistol out. He set it on the table in front of him, the barrel pointed at Slocum, the judge's hand still on the butt of the little Smith & Wesson .38, much like the bellygun Slocum carried inside his belt.

"I'm not going to shoot you, Judge," Slocum said.

"No, but if you don't sit down right this minute, I might shoot you where you stand and rule it self-defense."

Slocum hesitated.

The judge picked up the pistol again, aimed it at Slocum and cocked the hammer back.

The clicking sounded loud in the silence of the room.

The judge's finger curled around the trigger and his mouth stopped worrying the stub of cigar poking from between his grotesque little lips.

7

Slocum sat down, his face impassive.

The judge put the pistol back in its drawer, smiled.

"You see, John Slocum, I know who you are. You don't remember me, do you?"

Slocum shook his head.

"I've put on some poundage since the war, lost some hair on my pate, shaved off my beard. But I remember you, all right, and I know you're a wanted man back in Georgia. Calhoun County, I believe. I think the sheriff has a flyer on you somewhere in his office."

"I don't remember you," Slocum said.

"No, perhaps not. But I served under General Sterling Price, same as you. I believe General Lee made you a courier after Grant took Vicksburg, am I right?"

Slocum nodded.

"You came with quite a reputation. And after you rode with Quantrill, that reputation began to grow."

"I didn't come to your court to swap war stories, Judge."

"No, indeed you did not. From what I understand, you are here to testify on behalf of the accused."

"He's an innocent man."

The judge's face flushed a rosy hue and his protruding eyes flashed with a sudden rage.

"I am the judge here. Not you, John Slocum. I decide who's innocent or guilty."

"I was an eyewitness to that murder last night. I saw . . ."

The judge raised the flat of his hand to stop Slocum from saying another word.

"Just hold on, Slocum. I'm not taking testimony here. I just wanted to remind you that you're a stranger here and might be stepping into something you can't handle. You may have thought you saw something last night, when in fact, you had been drinking strong spirits and might have been mistaken. We treat eyewitnesses with a great deal of skepticism here in Del Rio."

"I see," Slocum said, knowing he was not going to get anywhere with Judge Wyman. Not here. Not now. He studied the man behind the desk, trying to picture him as he once might have been: in uniform, younger, with hair on his head, leaner. General Lee had appointed Slocum to be his courier to General Price. If Wyman had been with Price, he should remember him. Price had been the man who had sent him to join Quantrill, before Lawrence, before Bloody Kansas. Yes, he should remember him. He did remember him.

"You were Price's adjutant," Slocum said.

"Aide-de-camp."

"You gave me a hard time. Why?"

Wyman glowered at Slocum.

"You were just a raw kid, a country boy, back then."

"You got something against country boys?"

"I thought you were favored by General Lee because of what your father did at Manassas. William Slocum, wasn't that his name?"

"My father was killed at Manassas."

"I know. That was part of it. He commanded the militia out of Georgia. I knew him. I didn't think he was a hero, like they said. Got killed by a minie ball, I believe."

"He was a hero to me, and so was my brother, Robert."

"Robert Slocum. Yes, I heard about him, too. He was with Stonewall Jackson. Got killed at Gettysburg leading a charge. A failed charge, I believe."

"That was Pickett's fault. My brother fought bravely."

"Well, I was the one who asked General Price to put you under Quantrill's command. You fit the kind of men he had in his outfit. Rabble, if you ask me."

"So, now you're still giving me a hard time, is that it, Wyman?"

"That's Judge Wyman to you, Slocum. No. The war's over. But you went back to Calhoun Country down in Georgia and raised hell."

"The damned carpetbaggers stole my pa's property, cleaned us out. I killed a crook. In self-defense."

"You killed a judge, Slocum."

Wyman's eyes flashed a blazing hatred that seemed to flare up in him like a flash fire in a greasy skillet.

"A crooked judge, who stole my family's land."

"The law has a long memory, Slocum. Before you testify here today, I just wanted you to know where you stand with me."

"You've made it pretty clear, Judge."

"Good. Just so we understand each other."

Slocum stood up, knowing that he was about to be dismissed. He looked down at Judge Wyman, who was still seated at his desk.

"Do you believe in justice, Judge?" Slocum asked.

"That's why I'm a judge."

"Then, that's all I need to know. Is the accused going to get a jury trial?"

"No."

"Fine. Then, if you mete out justice, you have nothing to worry about."

"What are you getting at, Slocum? Are you threatening me?"

"No, Judge. I'm just watching you."

"Get the hell out of here. The bailiff will call you when it's your turn to testify."

Slocum did not reply. He turned on his heel and walked out. The bailiff was standing just outside the judge's door, one hand resting on the butt of his pistol.

"Expecting trouble?" Slocum asked innocently.

"Follow me outside the courtroom," the bailiff said, never batting an eye.

Slocum sat outside with Carmen. She asked him what had happened inside.

"Just a friendly talk with the judge," he said.

"Friendly?"

"Not really, Carmen. He's trying to scare me off from testifying on your brother's behalf."

"But you will do this?"

"I will testify as to what I saw last night. Yes."

"Good."

They did not have to wait long. Slocum heard the judge call the courtroom to order and then he heard the murmurings of the prosecuting attorney, followed by a more subdued voice extolling the virtues of the accused, who had no prior criminal record.

The bailiff came through the doors and beckoned to Carmen, who followed him inside. Slocum strained to hear the questioning and her answers, but the voices were too muffled. Then it was quiet. He waited for Carmen to return, but she did not. He heard arguing from inside the courtroom and then it was quiet once again, for a few moments.

The bailiff came for Slocum and he went inside the courtroom. He was sworn in and took the witness chair. He looked over at the defendant's table and saw Luis Delgado sitting with his attorney. Behind him, Carmen sat, a worried look on her face. Delgado's eyes seemed full of pleading as he returned Slocum's gaze and John thought that the trial had probably not been going his way.

The defense attorney introduced himself as Emory Davis. The prosecutor's name was LeRoy Richards and when he spoke, Slocum could almost see him drooling, so eager was he for a conviction. At any cost.

"Mr. Slocum," Davis began, "you were at the Del Rio Hotel last night?"

"I was."

"Do you see anyone you recognize from last night now here in the courtroom?"

"I do."

"Could you point that person out for the court, please?"

Slocum pointed to Delgado.

"Let the record show that the witness pointed to the defendant, Luis Delgado."

A woman sitting in front of the bench wrote something down in a ledger. Slocum wondered if it was shorthand and if it was accurate.

"Now, tell us what you saw last night, anything that involved the defendant."

Slocum told what he had seen. He described the mysterious veiled woman, the dancing, the fatal shot. He said that he saw the woman hand the smoking pistol to the defendant.

"So, a woman shot Mr. Granby?"

"Objection," Richards interjected. "If the person wore a veil, the witness could not know for sure if Luis Delgado was dancing with a woman or a male accomplice."

"Sustained," Judge Wyman said, his face a mask of inscrutability.

"Did you see the person hand the pistol to the defendant?" Davis asked.

"Yes. I did. And it was a woman. And she then ran out of the dining room."

The prosecutor was on his feet with another objection.

"Sustained," the judge said. "Strike the phrase 'And, it was a woman.' "

"Your Honor," Davis said, "this is crucial testimony from an eyewitness."

"He's not an expert on gender," the judge said, glancing at Richards.

"Well, he damned well may be," Davis said.

The judge pounded his gavel on the block of wood sitting on his bench.

"That it, Emory?" Wyman asked.

"Your witness," Davis said. He walked to the defense table and sat down. Richards got up and walked up close to Slocum.

"Mr. Slocum," Richards said, "are you a drinking man? Do you imbibe strong spirits upon occasion?"

"You could say that."

"I just did. Answer the question, please."

"Yes. I sometimes imbibe strong spirits." Slocum's mouth curved in a wry smile.

"And were you drinking spirits last night when you saw the defendant dancing with someone?"

"I had a drink or two."

"Were you drunk?"

"No," Slocum said.

"Did you see someone shoot Mr. Granby?"

"I did."

"It happened fast, did it not?" Richards said.

"Pretty fast."

"Perhaps too fast for you to see who fired the shot."

"No, I saw the woman fire the shot into Mr. Granby's heart. She was very deliberate."

"I move that the court strike the last response," Richards said.

"I object," Davis said, rising to his feet. "The witness is testifying under oath. The court should recognize that Mr. Slocum is speaking the truth. And that truth is evidence."

"I'll decide what is evidence," Judge Wyman said, and Slocum knew that the trial in the case of Del Rio versus Luis Delgado was going downhill. Delgado was sweating and so was his attorney, Emory Davis.

Somewhere in the wings, Slocum knew, the hangman was waiting.

8

Slocum listened to the attorneys wrangle with the judge for several minutes and was once again reminded of why he had fled Calhoun County in his native Georgia after shooting, in self-defense, a crooked judge who had stolen his land. He knew he'd get no justice if he'd been arrested.

He also knew that a man like Luis Delgado, all alone, falsely accused, stood little chance of getting justice in a town like Del Rio where Mexicans were treated worse than second-class citizens. He had seen many border towns, and they were all pretty much the same. The white townsfolk treated Mexicans and others with darker skins, little better than dogs. Slocum was getting a very bad feeling about Del Rio and its court, presided over by Judge Andrew J. Wyman.

Finally, the issues were resolved by the judge and Slocum faced the prosecuting attorney, who proceeded to try and destroy the eyewitness testimony even further.

"Mr. Slocum, when a firearm is discharged, there is considerable smoke issuing from the muzzle, is that correct?"

"Sometimes."

"What do you mean *sometimes*?"

"It depends on the load, the amount of powder behind the bullet."

"Does a small pistol produce a lot of smoke?"

"Sometimes, depending on the caliber."

The defense attorney objected.

"Mr. Slocum is not a firearms expert," Davis said.

The judge turned to Slocum, looked at him for several seconds and then turned back to the defense attorney.

"Overruled. Mr. Richards, why don't you ask Mr. Slocum if he's an expert on firearms?"

The prosecutor smiled at this small victory.

"Mr. Slocum, are you an expert on firearms?"

"No, sir. Not an expert."

"But you have discharged a number of firearms, haven't you? Weren't you in the war? Didn't you learn to shoot a Colt .45 when you were a cavalryman with Quantrill's Raiders?"

The defense objected.

The judge overruled.

"Answer the question," Wyman said to Slocum.

"I learned how to use the Colt .45, yes."

"And when you fired that Colt, it made a lot of smoke, right?"

"There's always smoke when you burn powder," Slocum said.

"Now, to last night. Is it possible that when the shot was fired that killed Mr. Granby, there was so much smoke that you could not tell who fired the pistol?"

"No," Slocum said. "That's not true. I saw the woman fire the shot that killed Granby. Then she gave the pistol to the defendant there."

"This mysterious woman?"

"Yes. She wore a veil. I could not see her face."

The prosecutor snorted in derision and waved an arm through the air as if dismissing all of Slocum's testimony.

"I have no further questions of this witness," he said and sat down.

"You may step down, Mr. Slocum," Wyman said.

Slocum left the witness stand and sat in the courtroom next to Carmen.

"Call your next witness," Wyman said to the defense attorney.

"I have no further witnesses," the defense attorney said.

"Very well, then. Mr. Prosecutor, you may proceed."

"I call Cordelia Granby to the stand."

The bailiff left the courtroom. When he reentered, Mrs. Granby followed him. She was escorted by Bill Hardesty. In fact, she had her arm in his. He gave her arm a squeeze as she walked up behind the bailiff to the witness stand. Hardesty sat in the front row. Slocum wondered if he was just being kind to the recently widowed woman or if there was something more between the two. Cordelia sat down and was sworn in, but her gaze remained fixed on Hardesty. And, unless Slocum was mistaken, her look was laden with lust.

The prosecutor took Cordelia through the usual qualifying questions and then asked her if she had seen the shooting. She said she had not actually seen the shooting, but she said when her husband was struck with the bullet that killed him, she had looked up and seen the Mexican man standing there with a smoking pistol in his hand. She had not seen a woman wearing a veil.

Slocum thought she either must have been coached by the prosecuting attorney, or she was lying through her teeth.

The defense attorney couldn't shake Cordelia from her testimony and Cordelia was dismissed. She sat down with

Hardesty and they moved very close together, one of his hands on her leg, and her hand in his, as if they had been longtime lovers.

The prosecutor called several other eyewitnesses, who said that the Mexican, Luis Delgado, had shot Granby. These were waiters and diners who said they had been at the Del Rio Hotel the night before, but Slocum knew damned well that none of them had been anywhere near Granby when he was shot.

Slocum leaned over and whispered in Carmen's ear. "I've seen railroad jobs before, but this one takes the cake."

"What is this railroad job?" she asked.

"For some reason, the judge, the town—somebody— wants to hang your brother. This is not a fair trial."

"What can I do?" she asked.

"I don't know," Slocum said. "In some states, I think you can appeal the death penalty. Del Rio is so far off the beaten path, and Judge Wyman seems to have such control, that his decision is probably final and can't be changed."

Carmen's eyes misted over and she grabbed Slocum's arm, squeezed it tightly.

"*Dios mio*," she said. Then she crossed herself and Slocum breathed a deep sigh.

"The court finds the defendant guilty of murder in the first degree," Judge Wyman said.

"Will the defendant stand up?" the bailiff beseeched. "You will now hear the sentence of the court."

Slocum shook his head at the swiftness of the decision. He studied Wyman's face to see if there was even an ounce of compassion or understanding in the man. Wyman's face was a rigid noncommittal mask. Only his eyes flashed a warning that the sentence was bound to be harsh.

Wyman pounded his gavel to silence the ripple of murmurs in the courtroom.

"The court hereby sentences you, Luis Delgado, to death. You will, at noon today, hang by the neck until you are dead. May Almighty God have mercy on your soul."

Delgado crumpled in his chair. His head dropped down to his chest in defeat. His body shook with sudden sobs. Carmen began to weep as well. She turned to Slocum and buried her head on his chest. He put an arm around her and held her to him while she vented her grief and anger.

The courtroom came to life, then, as Judge Wyman left the bench and returned to his chambers. The defense attorney got up and shook the prosecutor's hand, but there was no warmth in the gesture. Then, Emory Davis turned back to his client, who was now sitting up straight, wiping his eyes. The bailiff appeared behind him with a pair of handcuffs and tapped him on the top of the head.

Delgado stood up and put his arms behind him. The bailiff cuffed him. Luis turned and looked at his sister, his lips moving with a silent message. It was in Spanish, but Slocum knew what he was saying. *"Lo siento."* "I am sorry," Luis said.

"I love you, my brother," Carmen replied in audible Spanish, and then watched helplessly as her brother was led away.

"I'm sorry, too," Slocum said.

"I will go to see my brother now. It is not long until they will hang him."

"No, you go ahead. If there's anything I can do . . ."

His voice trailed off as Carmen stood up, her eyes wet with tears, her face strained. But she stood proudly and walked out of the courtroom alone. Slocum arose from his seat and looked over at Bill Hardesty and Cordelia

Granby. They both were smiling and they embraced as if they were celebrating a victory.

Slocum looked around for Lorelei, to see if she had been in the courtroom, but he saw no sign of her. He wondered if she knew that her father was with Cordelia, and if she did know, he wondered if she approved of their relationship.

It was not his business, Slocum knew, but he wondered now if Cordelia herself had had anything to do with her husband's death.

Hardesty saw Slocum and waved to him. Jubilantly, Slocum thought.

Slocum turned away and walked from the courtroom, an anger blazing in him that had, in the past, turned dangerous for many of those who had incurred his wrath.

Hardesty and Cordelia caught up to Slocum outside the courtroom.

"John," Hardesty called, "wait up."

Slocum stopped and turned to face Hardesty.

"What do you think?" Hardesty asked.

"About what?"

"About the judge's decision. The sentence."

"I thought it was about right for a kangaroo court down in backwoods Georgia."

Cordelia, who stood beside Hardesty, glared at Slocum. Her eyes were cold, lifeless. Her lips pursed slightly and drained of color.

"But justice was served," Hardesty said.

Slocum's eyes narrowed to dark slits.

"Was it, Hardesty? For whom? Certainly not for that poor innocent Mexican who was set up for that murder last night. All he gets out of this is a rope he doesn't deserve."

"Mr. Slocum," Cordelia said. "That man murdered my husband. I want to see him hang for his crime."

"Ma'am," Slocum said. "I'll bet you'd like to put the rope around his neck, wouldn't you?"

"How dare you," Cordelia exclaimed.

"That's enough, Slocum," Hardesty said, turning cold. "See you at the hanging."

"I'll be there," Slocum said.

"And then you'll be on your way, out of Del Rio," Hardesty said.

Slocum fixed him with a frosty stare.

"Not by a long shot, Hardesty. I aim to stick around and get to the bottom of this. Maybe you ought to be the one to ride out of Del Rio. While you still can."

Hardesty grabbed Cordelia by the arm and the two strode away angrily.

Slocum watched them go.

But he knew he had struck a nerve.

9

Slocum waited outside the jail. When the bailiff emerged, he approached the man, who stared at Slocum with undisguised belligerence.

"A word with you, Bailiff."

"We got nothing to talk about, Slocum. Trial's over."

"You'll talk to me, Rufus Early, unless you want to eat about six inches of gun barrel."

"You threatenin' me?"

"As I would any thick-necked bully wearing a badge and totin' a billy club," Slocum said, his gaze unwavering, his jaw set to a granite hardness.

"Well, what in hell do you want? I got things to do before the noon hangin'."

"I want to know why you picked up Luis Delgado and paid him to go to the Del Rio Hotel last night."

"I didn't do no such thing."

"If you lie to me, I'll seriously consider giving you a drubbing right here and now."

"Damn you, Slocum. What I do is none of your damned business."

"It's my business when I see a man railroaded in a courtroom and sent to his death without just cause."

"You'll have to take that up with Judge Wyman."

"I'm taking it up with you, Early. Now, who paid you to pick up Luis Delgado?"

The bailiff broke out in a sweat. Beads of moisture filled the furrows on his forehead and streaks of perspiration coursed down from his sideburns, glistened in the sun like streaks of liquid mica.

Slocum took hold of the man's right arm at the elbow and ushered him to a space between the jail and another building. There, he reached down and grabbed Early by the scrotum. He squeezed.

Veins popped out in the bailiff's neck and he grunted in pain, doubled over. Slocum increased the pressure.

"Now, let's hear the truth," Slocum said. "Who paid you to pick up Delgado and bring him into town."

"Stop," the bailiff pleaded. "All right. I'll tell you. But I know nothing else."

Slocum released his hold on the bailiff's testicles and stepped back. Early straightened up, his face now covered with a sheen of sweat, his shirt soaked through with perspiration.

"Let's hear it, Early."

"All I know is the hangman's wife asked me to invite Delgado to meet her at the Del Rio. She said she'd pay him to dance with her."

"What's her name?"

"Pandora."

"Pandora?"

"Pandora Fernandez. She's married to the hangman, Carlos Fernandez. You'll see 'em both at the hanging. You can ask her about it."

"If she's the one who danced with Luis Delgado," Slocum said, "then, she's the one who murdered Granby."

"I wouldn't know."

"No, you probably wouldn't and that's why I'm not going to beat you within an inch of your life. You can go now, but you haven't heard the last of me."

"Slocum, I know you've already had a passel of advice, but here's some more for you."

"Make it quick."

"Del Rio looks like a nice town, but it's got an ugly underbelly. There are people here you just don't want to cross. And people you don't want to deal with. There's a lot at stake here and Granby's murder might just be the first of others."

"What in hell are you talking about?" Slocum asked.

"That land Granby wanted to buy. It's blood land and there'll be more spilled before it's over."

"Blood land?"

"That's all I'm going to tell you. That's all I know. Granby wasn't the onliest man who wanted to buy it. And he didn't even know what was on it."

"Do you?"

"No. But there's something about that land that will get a man killed if he finds out what it is."

Slocum swore.

"You watch yourself, Slocum. It won't be me comin' after you. But mark my words. Somebody will if you keep pokin' your nose into this business."

Slocum let Rufus Early go and then stepped out from between the two buildings, into the sunlight.

A few blocks away, he heard voices rising in pitch. He saw people walking toward the center of town. They looked, he thought, like people going to a pie social. They were in no hurry, but they were all streaming to the town square, the place where Luis Delgado would hang by the neck until dead.

Slocum walked down the street to a general store, went inside and bought a dozen cheroots. Outside, he lit one and then walked slowly toward the middle of Del Rio, taking his time. He puzzled over what he had learned from Rufus Early and wondered how Bill Hardesty fit in to the intrigue he had wandered into the night before. One thing was sure. Granby's widow, Cordelia, was in it up to her neck. And now, the hangman's wife, Pandora, who must have some connection to both Cordelia Granby and Bill Hardesty.

For a moment, Slocum considered just walking away, riding back north and leaving the mess in Del Rio for others to untangle.

And then he thought of Carmen Delgado and knew that, for her sake, he had to find out the truth.

Just before noon, the main street of Del Rio began to fill with people who had heard about the hanging of Luis Delgado.

Slocum strolled onto the edge of the crowd, a striking figure in his black frock coat and tall, lean figure. He saw Mexican women wearing black dresses with their rosaries in gnarled hands, saying their beads, their lips moving silently in prayer. There were seedy-looking men with gaunt, unshaven faces and dirty shirts, sipping from flasks, their eyes out of focus and watery from whiskey and sleeplessness. And there were men and women who were dressed well, a woman with a parasol shading her young scrubbed face and the man next to her in a banker's suit, with not a wrinkle in it, and a derby perched atop his head.

Then Slocum spotted Carmen standing with a small group of people near the scaffold, a black lace shawl covering her head, a rosary in her hand, a flower pinned to her dark blouse. An old woman, her face wrinkled with age, stood next to her, and the two were surrounded by wide-eyed urchins with bewildered, curious faces, as if they had been snatched from some dark room and placed in a sunlit place where the aroma of death was as thick as morning fog along the Rio Grande.

Carmen beckoned to Slocum, he thought, or perhaps she was just acknowledging his presence with a wave of her hand. He hesitated, unsure of her gesture, wondering whether he should stay where he was or walk over to her and be by her side. Then she made her intentions clear. She held out one hand and opened and closed it, indicating that she wanted him to come over.

Slocum made his way through the crowd and stood facing Carmen.

"This is my mother, Remedios," Carmen said. "Mama, this is John Slocum, the man I told you about."

"*Con mucho gusto*," Remedios said, pain flickering in her eyes like a smoking candle.

"I am glad you came, John," Carmen said. "It is almost unbearable to be here. But I wish my brother to see us here before he goes to heaven."

"I'm sorry, Carmen. I know it's tough. I wish there was something I could do."

A dog ran out onto the square and two boys chased it away with sticks. A street vendor passed by, pulling a cart with a burro. He stopped and people gathered around, buying hot tamales, *churros* and other treats. The sun reached its zenith and burned overhead.

A murmur arose among the crowd and Slocum felt Carmen tug at his arm. He looked up. A man walked across the street and people parted to let him through. But the man was not alone. A woman walked with him. She was slender and graceful and poised. The man wore a black morning coat and stovepipe boots. And he carried a thick heavy rope coiled up and hanging from his shoulder.

"That is the hangman," Carmen whispered.

"And is the woman with him his wife?"

"Yes, I think so."

Carmen shaded her eyes and peered at the woman.

"Yes," she said. "That is Pandora."

Slocum looked hard at the woman as she passed fairly close to them. There was something familiar about her. Her facial structure reminded him of someone, but he couldn't place the resemblance right away. She walked with a slink, as a cougar walks, self-assured, graceful, with no wasted movement.

At the scaffold, the woman stopped. The hangman climbed the steps and threw the rope over the beam. Then he tied off the bitter end to one of the supporting posts. There was no trapdoor and Slocum wondered why until he saw a man come up with a team of mules and tie ropes to the platform, ropes that were secured to yokes on the mules' shoulders. Then he noticed the wood blocks under the wheels of the scaffold, chocks that kept the platform stationary.

So, Slocum realized, the mules would just pull the platform away, leaving the condemned man dangling there with a broken neck. He shuddered at the thought and turned his gaze once again toward the woman he knew as Pandora.

To Slocum's surprise, she was looking at him, too. She stared straight at him with piercing eyes, eyes that also seemed familiar to him.

Pandora stared at Slocum.

And then she smiled.

The smile was almost demonic, he thought.

The smile sent a cold shiver up Slocum's spine.

The hangman's lady. She was enjoying this macabre spectacle of death in a public square.

And she wanted Slocum to know that she enjoyed watching a man hang by her husband's manila rope.

10

Pandora turned away from Slocum and waited, as her husband joined her. The hangman took his wife to a place near the scaffold, kissed her and then walked toward Slocum as if a meeting had been prearranged. Carmen shrank back, and so did her mother.

"John Slocum, I presume. Your name keeps coming up. I'm Carlos Fernandez, and I welcome you to the festivities here in Del Rio."

Fernandez held out his hand. Slocum didn't shake it.

"Very well. I just wanted to say that I'm looking forward to meeting you again, Slocum. At the top of that scaffold there. You have a good long neck. Strong. The kind I like."

"What kind of a bastard are you, Fernandez?"

Fernandez smiled.

"I imagine the same kind you are, you rednecked piece of southern trash."

The smile stayed on the hangman's face.

"Maybe we will be seeing each other again," Slocum said. "Only you'll be up there on that scaffold by yourself, with one of your own nooses around your neck."

"Don't count on it. I see your kind all the time in my profession. You ride into town and you either die of lead poisoning or I snap your neck like a twig."

"I wouldn't be a bit surprised to see your lovely wife dangling at the end of one of your ropes when this is over."

"You son of a bitch."

"Is this the pot calling the kettle black?" Slocum said.

"You go to hell, Slocum. I hope you enjoy seeing a preview of your own grisly death."

With that, the hangman turned on his heel and marched back to the scaffold. Moments later, Slocum heard a commotion and turned to see the crowd parting once again as the bailiff and two other armed guards, both carrying Winchesters, both flanking Luis Delgado, walked across the plaza, heading for the scaffold.

A hush fell over the crowd for those few moments. People in the crowd stretched their necks, straining to see the accused murderer who was about to meet his maker. Carmen grabbed Slocum's arm and squeezed it with both hands. Her mother began to weep quietly. She crossed herself and her lips moved in a silent prayer.

Delgado was led up the steps to the platform. Slocum could see that his legs were wobbly and that he was shaking all over. He stumbled at the top step and the crowd gasped as if that were the first of many dramatic moments to come.

Delgado's hands were tied behind him and the two guards wrestled him into position beneath the dangling rope. Then, Fernandez climbed the steps and spoke to the hapless Mexican. Delgado's lips remained tightly pursed. He did not speak. Instead, he gazed down at his sister and mother. Slocum saw tears ooze from his eyes and trickle down his cheeks.

Then the hangman reached inside his morning coat and

produced a black hood, which he placed over Delgado's head. Carmen let out a soft scream. Her mother sobbed loudly as the hangman pulled the rope down and placed it around the young man's neck, making sure the knotted portion was just under Delgado's left ear.

Next, the bailiff walked up the steps to the platform, carrying a sheet of paper in his hand.

Rufus Early read the judge's death sentence aloud to the silent, attentive crowd. He seemed to enjoy his role in the macabre ceremony. When he was finished he descended the steps and stood watching. The two guards, whom Slocum now recognized as sheriff's deputies, "Smitty" Smith and Larry Jones, nodded to Fernandez and then left the scaffold, joining the bailiff.

Finally, Fernandez walked down the steps and took a position near the mule driver, who sat on his seat, whip in hand, ready to strike the rumps of the two animals hitched to the platform.

The crowd went silent again, waiting for Fernandez to give the signal.

The hangman glanced over his shoulder one last time at Delgado and then raised his arm. He brought it down swiftly and suddenly.

The driver cracked the whip and snapped the reins across the backs of the two mules and they surged in their traces, jerking the platform forward.

A collective cry arose from the crowd as the platform rolled away, out from under Delgado. He dropped straight down until the rope stopped his progress. There was a snapping sound as the prisoner's neck broke and then he was kicking in the throes of death, his body turning around, his head at an angle.

Carmen collapsed against Slocum and he put his arm around her to hold her up. Her mother dropped to her knees, sobbing and praying, crossing herself, unable to look at the body of her son twisting slowly at the end of the rope, his feet just twitching slightly.

Slocum looked at Pandora, who stood there, staring at the dead man. She wasn't grinning, but there was a smile of satisfaction on her face. The sight sent a cold chill up Slocum's spine.

The two deputies stood by until the hangman signaled to someone Slocum couldn't see. A few seconds later, two Mexicans rolled a handcart out from between two buildings and headed for the scaffold. A freshly made pine box rode atop the cart. The two deputies stepped out and walked over to the scaffold. One of them climbed the stairs while the other waited just below the body of Luis Delgado.

The man atop the platform, Smitty, held onto the rope, while the hangman walked around behind the scaffold and began untying the rope that had secured it to one of the posts. When the rope was slack, Smitty slowly lowered the body until the two Mexicans grabbed Delgado's sides. Then Smitty let out the slack.

Jones helped the two Mexicans load the body into the coffin. He was the one who removed the rope from around Delgado's neck, handling it gingerly, as if it was a poisonous snake. Jones held it aloft until the hangman came and coiled it up neatly, slung it over his shoulder.

After the cart pulled away, heading for the undertaker's, Slocum saw the banker, Rankins, for the first time. He had walked over to Hardesty and Cordelia, stood talking to them. Slocum looked around for Lorelei, but he didn't see her. Perhaps, he thought, a hanging was more than she could stomach.

"John, will you come to the funeral for my brother?" Carmen asked.

"Yes. When is it?"

"Two days from now, I think. It is so sad. I must leave and take my mother home now."

"Do you know those two Mexicans who took your brother away?"

"Yes. They are friends. They will wait until the . . . the body . . . the remains . . . are prepared and bring my brother to our house. You can come by, if you wish. We will have food and drink for those who come to pay their respects."

"I don't know where you live, Carmen."

"It is a little village east of town. It is called Hidalgo. I will send someone to the hotel. He will bring you to our house when we are ready."

"Fair enough," Slocum said.

He watched her and her mother walk through the thinning crowd. Then they disappeared as people wandered to and fro, talking of the hanging among themselves, their voices low and whispery as if the spirit of the dead man lingered on in the very air they breathed.

Rankins, Hardesty and Cordelia walked toward the bank as if they had a prearranged meeting there, and Slocum started walking toward the hotel. He would have to get another room, or move his gear somewhere else. His bedroll and rifle were still in Lorelei's room. There were some other things he wanted to do, as well, ask some questions, find out where the land lay that Granby had wanted to buy before he was killed.

His path crossed that of Pandora and Carlos Fernandez, who were walking away from the place where the scaffold had been. The platform had already been moved back into the space between two buildings, out of sight and out of mind. Neat and tidy, Slocum thought. No sign of the horror that had occurred in the center of town, back to business as usual.

"Did you enjoy the show, Slocum?" Fernandez said.

"Fernandez, you remind me of two or three men I knew in the war. These men were in a special classification."

"Oh, what classification was that?"

"We called them cowards."

"I am not a coward."

"No? What do you call a man who murders innocent men who can't fight back? What do you call a man who preys on his victims while they're tied up and can't hurt him? I call such a man not only a coward, but a man with snakes inside his heart, snakes that fill him with a poison every time his heart pumps."

"Slocum, you're so full of shit, you stink."

"You watch out for those snakes, Fernandez. One day, they'll get loose and crawl all through your innards, clear up to your brain."

"Maybe I'll see you bye and bye, Slocum. Then we'll see who the damned coward is."

With that, Fernandez and Pandora walked away. She shot Slocum a dirty look and then her mouth bent in that smug smile of hers that was as cold as the frozen grimace on a dead woman's face, as lifeless as a mouth painted on a mask.

Slocum turned to walk back toward the Del Rio Hotel when he heard a man's voice call his name.

"Hold up, Mr. Slocum."

Slocum stopped and turned around. Hurrying toward him was a man he recognized, a man he had seen only that morning.

"A word with you, please, Mr. Slocum," Emory Davis said. There was an anxious look on his face, which surprised Slocum.

"Sure," Slocum said. "What's on your mind, Mr. Davis?"

"Will you walk with me to my office? I have some things to tell you."

"About Luis Delgado?"

"No. I'm sorry he was convicted. I feel badly about that young man being hanged when I know in my heart he was innocent."

"Well, we have some common ground."

"Yes. I think we might have more common ground."

Davis looked around furtively as if he were afraid of being overheard, or even being seen with Slocum.

"It won't take long. But what I have to say might be important. I know there's nothing we can do to bring Luis back, but maybe we can . . . maybe you can . . ."

And then Davis just stopped, as if he was afraid to say any more just then.

"Mr. Davis," Slocum said, "are you afraid of something? Or someone?"

Davis sucked in a quick breath. And then his eyes turned smoky as if some darkness in him had risen up and threatened to turn him blind as a stone.

"Come with me, will you, Mr. Slocum? We can't talk here."

The smoke in Davis's eyes cleared and was replaced by a look Slocum knew only too well. In the lawyer's eyes there was the look of fear, a fear so great it seemed to grip the man's throat and render him speechless while draining all the color from his face.

11

Emory Davis had a small office near the courthouse on a little side street where there were other little adobe offices with false fronts bearing such signs as *Abogado*, Notary Public, Land and Assayers. There was a county map on the wall and a certificate of the law degree Davis had earned at a university in Tennessee, one that Slocum had never heard of, but which looked genuine. He had a desk, three chairs, a filing cabinet and an old safe piled high with papers. Bookshelves lined the empty wall space and these were crammed full of law books.

"Have a seat, Mr. Slocum," Davis said as he sat behind his cluttered desk, which was a flat door propped up by boxes.

Slocum sat down, pulled out two cheroots. He offered one to Davis, who shook his head. But the attorney pushed a large clay *cenicero* closer to the edge of his desk nearest Slocum.

"Here's an ashtray," Davis said.

Slocum struck a lucifer and lighted his cheroot. He blew out the match and placed it in the ashtray.

"Sorry you lost the case, Mr. Davis. An innocent man was hanged today."

"I know. I feel badly about that. I was assigned to Delgado just before the trial. I believed he was innocent."

"I know he was."

"Unfortunately, your testimony didn't convince Judge Wyman. But that's not why I asked you here. What's done is done. We can't undo it."

Slocum drew on the cheroot and looked at Davis, wondering what was on his mind. The man was nervous, jumpy. As if he expected the door to burst open at any moment with an assassin standing there, gun in hand, to kill him.

"What, then?" Slocum asked.

"Just before the trial began, my life was threatened," Davis said. "The bailiff handed me an envelope." Davis reached over to a stack of papers and lifted off an envelope. He opened it, pulled out a piece of paper and stood up to hand it to Slocum.

Slocum read the short note.

"Lose this Delgado case or die," the note read. It was unsigned. It was written in flowery Spenserian script. A woman, perhaps? Slocum wondered. He handed the note back to Davis.

"Well, you lost the case, Davis. So, you're safe, probably."

"Mr. Slocum, this isn't the first such note I've seen."

Slocum's eyebrows arched. He blew smoke out of his mouth.

"When I started here, I had a partner, Seth Brumley. He was killed a month ago. Murdered. He got a note just like this before he went to trial defending a man we believed to be innocent of theft and murder. The man was acquitted and when Seth left the courtroom, he was killed by a shotgun blast."

"Do you know who did it?"

Davis shook his head.

"A day later, the man who was acquitted was killed in the same way. I'm beginning to think there is no justice in Del Rio."

"Do you think Judge Wyman had anything to do with those killings?"

"I don't know what to think. I'm jumping at every shadow. I didn't want to take this Delgado case, but Wyman insisted. He said he would see to it that I lost my license to practice law if I didn't take it. So I did. But the case felt just like the one Seth handled. Behind both, there was the common denominator of a piece of land that has suddenly, inexplicably, become very valuable."

"I'm afraid you have me there. What piece of land is that?" Slocum asked.

"Actually, there are two pieces of land involved."

Davis got up from his desk and turned to the map on the wall, which showed all of Val Verde County and much of that part of Texas, as well. He pointed to the Rio Grande, which ran along the Mexican–United States border.

"We have to go back a ways, but I think you'll get the picture, Mr. Slocum. As you can see here, Del Rio is right smack dab at the confluence of the Rio Grande and San Felipe Creek, which runs into it."

"Yes," Slocum said. "I see it."

"Now, Bill Hardesty owns land up along San Felipe Creek, and the land that Mr. Granby wanted to buy borders the Rio Grande and runs at an angle that connects it to the creek. This parcel here is around one hundred thousand acres. It's worth a great deal of money."

"Why?"

"The Spaniards who settled on this side of the border founded Del Rio, but it was just a settlement until after the Civil War. Then, as Americans took up residence here, they realized that water in this part of Texas was in short supply. But they discovered, only recently, that San Felipe Springs, which feeds the creek, produces a bountiful water supply. Now some people, Hardesty among them, want to develop that stretch of creek and lure settlers here who will pay a premium for the land. They want to dig ditches and canals and irrigation aqueducts all along there. So the land represents a fortune for someone who is able to buy that one hundred thousand acres."

"I see," Slocum said.

"But that's not all. I'm afraid that there's another reason Hardesty wants to buy that land, and this just came up within the last few weeks—days—even."

"Before you say anything else," Slocum said, "why are you telling me these things? I don't live here. I have no stake in Del Rio."

"I've been asking myself the same question," Davis said. "I'll try and give you an answer."

Slocum waited while Davis collected his thoughts. Slocum could tell that the man had been worrying over this bone for some time, like a dog gnawing to get to the marrow.

"All towns are corrupt," Davis said. "And Del Rio is no exception. But the layers of deceit and corruption are so thick, so elaborate, that virtually nobody in town can see the decay underneath; and those that can don't want to see it. They just want to live in happy ignorance while the thieving and the lying washes over them like dirty water running down a gutter."

"You can spare me the philosophy, Mr. Davis."

"Please. Call me Emory. I'll get to the point, John, if I may address you that way."

Slocum nodded his approval.

"I watched you in court. I listened to you. And I checked up on you. You've got somewhat of a shady past, but you impress me as being an honest man. More than that, I believe you're a man with a code of honor that is rare in these parts, or anywhere else for that matter."

"You don't have to lay on the soft soap, Emory. I know who I am."

"Yes, of course." Davis paused, then went on. "Sometimes, a stranger can see things that the locals can't. You've landed in the middle of an ugly situation. By all rights, you should get on your horse and ride out of Del Rio and never give any of us another thought. But you're not going to do that, are you?"

"I don't know," Slocum said.

"I think your sense of justice compels you to stay."

"Or curiosity."

"No, it's more than curiosity, I think. Somebody wanted Delgado dead, John. Somebody tried to kill you."

"Do you know who that might be?" Slocum asked.

Davis shook his head.

"No, but I think you might find out. Sooner or later. Here's what I want you to know. What I found out. A few days ago, after Granby had expressed a strong interest in that one hundred thousand acres and planned to move his cattle operation from Colorado down here to Del Rio, a map and some documents surfaced. Well, they didn't surface, exactly, but Bill Hardesty stumbled on a strongbox buried on that property. He was looking it over for Granby, supposedly, and he found this strongbox. Inside, there was a map and a description of some gold buried by the Spaniards when they owned Texas."

"How did you find out about it?"

"The documents and the wording on the map were all in Spanish. A Spanish that is no longer spoken here and hasn't been spoken in a century or more on either side of the border. I am a scholar of Spanish history and the language. So, he came to me."

"And what did the documents and the map reveal?" Slocum asked.

Davis leaned forward and beckoned for Slocum to do the same.

"Hardesty swore me to secrecy, John," Davis whispered. "But because of what they did to Luis Delgado, I no longer feel bound by the oath I took."

"Go on," Slocum said.

"I translated manifests, lists, bills of lading and other lists, along with an account of how the gold came to be buried in dozens of different places along the Rio Grande, all on that one hundred thousand acres. But the directions for finding the gold were in the form of an intricate scheme that amounted to a puzzle. That puzzle has not been deciphered yet, but I know Hardesty wanted that land."

"Did Granby know about the gold?"

"No, not at first."

"How did he find out?"

"In an odd way," Davis said.

"Tell me," Slocum said.

"Hardesty went to Frank Rankins, the banker, and said that he wanted to buy the land, that he didn't want Rankins to loan Granby the money for the purchase. Rankins refused, because he didn't think Bill could pay such a large debt. Granby, Rankins said, was a good financial risk for the bank."

"That must have made Hardesty pretty mad."

"He let slip just enough to make Rankins suspicious. Hardesty told Rankins that once he owned the land, he would be able to pay it off within months, perhaps weeks. That made Rankins suspicious and one day he walked in on me while I was working on those translations and he saw enough to make him want in on the deal. Not with

Hardesty, but with Granby, who knew nothing about the treasure buried on the property."

"So, the circle widens," Slocum said.

"I finished the translation and was trying to work out the exact locations of the buried gold, in bullion form, when Hardesty demanded the documents be returned to him. So I surrendered them. I told Hardesty that he'd never find any of the gold, if it was still there, unless he could crack the code. Unknown to me, until after Hardesty left, was that someone was listening outside my window to our conversation. I had heard someone come in and then leave quickly."

"Do you know who it was?" Slocum asked. "Who was eavesdropping?"

"Not exactly."

"What do you mean by that?"

"I heard someone running away and I caught a glimpse of a long black skirt and when I went outside, I saw footprints outside my window."

"A woman?"

"Yes. A woman had overheard and now knew about the buried gold."

"Cordelia Granby?" Slocum offered.

Davis shook his head.

"No, it was not Cordelia. I checked my appointment book. No clue there. But I remembered a conversation I'd had the day before."

"And?"

"Pandora Fernandez had said she was coming to see me about something, and I completely forgot about it until that moment when I saw the shoe prints of a woman outside my window."

"So you think it was Pandora," Slocum said.

"I can't prove it. But, yes."

Slocum leaned back in his chair. The circle of those

who knew about the gold had indeed widened. If Pandora knew about it, perhaps she had approached Hardesty with a scheme.

"What are you thinking, John?"

"I'm thinking that I know why Luis Delgado was set up for the murder of Granby."

Davis let out a long sigh.

"If you do, your life is in even more danger than it was this morning, or last night."

"I know," Slocum said, taking a drag on his cheroot.

He had the feeling he was living on borrowed time.

12

Slocum stood up to leave Davis's office.

"Too bad you weren't able to keep copies of any of those documents," he said to Davis.

"Oh, but I did, John. They're right there in that safe."

Davis pointed to the safe. Slocum looked at it as if it were a bomb ready to explode.

"Isn't that taking a big risk, Emory?"

"I think I've almost got the riddle solved. When I do, I'm hoping you'll take the risk out of my hands."

"You hope too much," Slocum said.

Davis smiled and made a tent out of his hands as he leaned back in his chair.

"I'm betting you'll want what I have before you're through here in Del Rio. I've already contacted a friend in Austin, also a lawyer. We're preparing a case that will not only remove Judge Wyman from office, but get him and his fellow conspirators a long prison sentence."

"You think Wyman was in on the Granby murder?"

"I'd bet money on it."

"Can you prove it?"

Davis smiled.

"Not yet. But I also think you might be able to provide that proof."

"Don't bet on it," Slocum said, wryly. "Since you seem to be a betting man."

"We'll see, John. Good luck. We'll meet again, I'm sure."

"It seems to me, Emory, you're sure about too many things that are very uncertain."

Davis opened a desk drawer. Slocum heard the wood creak and whisper. He handed Slocum a folded piece of paper.

"What's this?" Slocum asked.

"That's a map of the one hundred thousand acres. It shows the Rio Grande and San Felipe Creek. In case you want to look around when you're not dodging bullets."

"Emory, I sense a frustrated man of adventure beneath that lawyer's suit you wear."

With that, Slocum put the folded map inside his frock coat pocket and left the attorney's office. He walked back to the hotel, went up to Lorelei's room. She opened the door and Slocum was shocked at her appearance. She seemed to have been crying. Her face was streaked with the tracks of tears, her hair disheveled and her clothing wrinkled, as if she had been lying down fully dressed.

Next to her, on the floor, was her bulging valise.

"Oh, it's you," she said. "I was just leaving."

"Where are you going?"

"Back home. To the ranch. I can't talk now. Your things are on the bed. I was going to tell the desk clerk when I checked out."

She looked distraught, distracted. She wouldn't look him square in the eye.

"What's wrong?" Slocum asked.

"I—I can't talk now. Please. I'm in a hurry."

"You weren't at the hanging," he said.

She flared up at him, her eyes wide and wild as if he had touched a nerve.

"That disgusting spectacle? No. Now, please get out of my way."

"Are you mad at me, Lorelei?" Slocum asked, stepping aside from her doorway.

She swept by him.

"No, not at you," she said, then broke into sobs. She doubled over for a second as she walked down the hall toward the stairs. Slocum started to go and help her, but she straightened up, held her head high and stormed away, leaving him confused and bewildered.

He waited, listening to her footfalls as she descended the stairs. They gradually faded away and Slocum shrugged, then entered the room. His gear was on the bed as Lorelei had said. He grabbed his bedroll, rifle and saddlebags, then walked from the room. He stopped at the desk in the lobby.

"Leaving us, Mr. Slocum?" the clerk said.

"Yes, but I wonder if you could answer a question for me."

"If I can," the clerk said. He was a man in his fifties with a bald pate, wearing a loud red vest and garter bands on his sleeves. He looked more like a gambler than a desk clerk.

"Can you tell me where the Hardesty ranch lies?"

"Why certainly. Miss Lorelei Hardesty just checked out. If you hurry, you might catch up to her."

"No, just give me the general directions on how to get to Bill Hardesty's ranch, if you would, please."

The clerk told him in a few sentences. In his mind, Slocum could picture it with the Rio Grande forming one border and the ranch crossing San Felipe Creek. Very close to the prime land that Granby had wanted to buy before he was murdered.

Slocum walked down to the stables, paid his bill and saddled up Ferro.

"You leavin' us, Slocum?" the stableman said.

"For a while. I might be back."

"Saw you at the hangin'. Was I you, I'd keep on ridin', right out of Del Rio."

"Oh? You know something I don't know?"

"No, sir. Just talk is all. You don't want to get on the wrong side of the judge and looks to me like you done did it."

"What's your name, feller?" Slocum asked.

"Raleigh Newsome. Raleigh as in *Sir Walter*."

"Well, Raleigh, maybe you can tell me about Judge Wyman and why I'm in his disfavor."

"No, sir, I can't tell you that."

"Why?"

" 'Cause people who buck the judge have a way of turnin' up at the end of a rope."

"Are you saying that the judge uses his office to kill his enemies?"

"Nope, ain't sayin' that at all, Mr. Slocum. It ain't the judge anyways. I mean, he stays to hisself. But he has others who do his dirty work for him."

"What others?"

Newsome looked around the barn as if to make sure nobody was listening to them. Still, he lowered his voice and stepped two paces closer to Slocum.

"Fernandez," he whispered, "and that bitch wife of his."

"The hangman? That's all he does, isn't it? Hang people?"

"He's hungry," Newsome said. "But that Pandora. She's even hungrier. She likes to watch men dangle at the end of a rope."

"Are you saying . . ."

"I'm saying, she's the one. She's the one who finds the victims. She sets them up. Wyman sentences them. And Carlos Fernandez carries out the sentence. So Pandora can watch."

Slocum swore under his breath.

"There have been others?" he asked.

"I can tell you some," Newsome said.

"Tell me."

"There was a Mexican caught stealing a cow. Only he didn't steal it. The cow was staked out. It had a brand. The Mex was leadin' the cow back to the ranch where it belonged. Suddenly, out of nowhere, here comes the sheriff, Curt Blandings, and his deputy, Smitty. They arrest the Mex and he hangs."

"Anybody else?"

"A drifter. I don't remember his name. He blew into town and got into a game of cards at a cantina. Pandora was there. She slipped a card into his pocket. The man was accused of cheating and somebody drew on him. The drifter shot, in self-defense. He was hanged, same as the others. One after another. A hanging a week. For months. And they all mentioned Pandora when they were being tried. Maybe not by name, but they said there was a woman there. The Mex said a woman told him about the cow what was staked out. Interestin', huh?"

"It's like watching a snake go after a mouse," Slocum said.

"You got that right, Slocum."

"Hasn't the town caught on? I mean, doesn't anyone speak up about these . . . these criminals?"

Newsome shook his head.

"One man did. A lawyer. He was convicted of murdering a little boy. They found the boy in his house, his throat cut. Nobody's spoke up since."

Slocum swore.

"I can hardly believe all this," he said.

"It's like a fever with them folks—Wyman and the Fernandezes. They got a taste of blood and they want more and more. I'm tellin' you, Slocum, they enjoy what they're doin'."

"I can see that there's never going to be any justice in this town as long as Wyman is judge and Fernandez is the hangman."

"And don't forget that Pandora. She's evil, that one."

Slocum said nothing. He said good-bye to Newsome and mounted Ferro.

"You comin' back or ridin' on?" Newsome asked.

"I don't know. I'll probably be back to board Ferro here."

"You'll stay at the Del Rio Hotel?"

"No. I don't know where I'll stay."

"Maybe out there at the cemetery, if you ain't careful."

"If it's my time," Slocum said and put the spurs to Ferro's flanks.

He knew he would stay around if for no other reason than to attend the wake for Carmen's brother. She said she'd send someone to get him and take him to the Mexican settlement, but now he knew he'd have to find it on his own. He didn't want to stay at the Del Rio again. He wanted to find some place out of the way, where it would take time for anyone to find him. And it would have to be a place he could defend easily, a place where he could see someone coming from a long way off.

One thing was sure. He wasn't going to let Hardesty, Wyman, Fernandez or any of the others involved get away with murder.

If he didn't stand up to the town, who would?

Nobody.

Slocum rode out of town by way of the backstreets so that he stood less chance of being seen by watchful eyes. He headed north along the Rio Grande. He wanted to see the land that Hardesty wanted to buy and take a look at his ranch. The first element of his plan to bring justice back to Del Rio meant learning the lay of the land. He knew he had enemies in town and maybe he would have to hide out for a time until he could gather enough evidence to send the murderers to prison.

And if he couldn't get the evidence, he would just have to draw everyone involved in the illegal hangings out in the open.

In the end, he knew he might have to play a waiting game—and then see who cracked first.

13

Slocum saw the name over the gate when he passed Hardesty's ranch. There was a symbol of a Rocking H brand beneath an arch that had the name Hardesty in big wooden letters over it. From the road, he could not see the ranch house, but the lane leading to it was plainly visible.

There were a few grazing cattle, almost as motionless as statues. In the air, there was the pungent aroma of alfalfa and lespedeza and the faint scent of clover. The sky was a yellow blaze on the western horizon, but clouds were building to the south, fluffy white ones that floated high above the river and the plain. A pair of swifts darted by on silent wings, and mourning doves whistled through the air like winged darts. It was a lonely, desolate place, for all that, and Slocum wondered why anyone would come to such a place and settle, so far from the hubs of commerce to the west and east.

He rode on, toward the one hundred thousand acres, referring to the map Davis had given him. There were a lot of hoofprints on the road, showing him evidence of horses both coming and going.

When he reached the acreage where the gold was supposedly buried, he saw that horses had left the road and ridden over the land there. He did not follow any of these, but, here and there, he saw signs of digging, as if someone had tried to follow the clues on the treasure map and had come up dry.

He thought of the futility of searching such a vast area for little caches of gold. Unless a man had an accurate map, he was unlikely to find anything beneath the ground except more dirt. It was odd, he thought, that men would kill to buy a piece of ground so large without knowing in advance where the treasure lay. But Slocum had long ago given up on trying to understand the stupidity and greed of some men, men who would go to any lengths to achieve wealth or a woman—without regard to the consequences.

He wondered, as he rode back along the road, what part Fernandez and his wife Pandora played in the scheme to acquire the land he rode upon. What connection did they have with Hardesty? And how much did Lorelei Hardesty know about her father and the widow Cordelia? Was she in on the scheme? She had been mighty upset about something when last he had seen her. Now, he wished he knew what had been bothering her.

He had no allies in Del Rio except for Emory Davis, and Davis, like everyone else, had his own personal axe to grind. He had lost a case and seen his client hanged. Now, perhaps, he wanted revenge. But Slocum knew how empty revenge could be. If it was a dish best served cold, then it was as tasteless as flat beer.

Just west of town, on the ride back to Del Rio, Slocum became aware that someone was following him. He didn't know who and he didn't know how many, but Ferro was as jittery as a long-tailed cat in a room full of rocking chairs. The horse kept turning its head and glancing, wide-eyed, at every dirt clod, his ears twisting in all directions, hardened to cones, trying to pick up any vagrant sound.

It was late afternoon and he had the sun at his back, a sun that was drifting down the western sky that was scudded with battens of clouds that were already rimmed with gold and salmon. If there was a rider behind him, where had he come from? The Hardesty ranch? Or was he just a traveler from the west, heading into Del Rio?

Slocum turned Ferro toward San Felipe Creek. There were trees there, cover. He had been riding out in the open and a good marksman with a long rifle could have picked him off easily once he came within range. He had no idea how far behind the rider was, but he knew the distance put him beyond the horizon because every time he turned around to look at his backtrail, he never saw the skyline broken by a man, or a woman, on horseback.

He reached the creek and found a stand of cottonwood trees that afforded him some protection from long-range rifle fire and a good view all around in case someone meant to sneak up on him. Slocum slipped his rifle from its sheath and laid it across his pommel, at the ready. Whoever was following him should show soon, he thought, and he'd have time to lever a cartridge into the chamber of his Winchester '73.

The minutes slipped by and the sun skidded farther down toward the horizon, drifting clouds hiding its blazing face every few minutes. Ferro pawed the ground with his right forefoot and continued to gaze westward, ears twitching, rubbery nostrils flexing to pick up any vagrant scent.

After a time, Slocum relaxed. Ferro had stopped fidgeting. The danger, if that had been what it was, had seemingly passed. Slocum picked up the rifle, hefted it in his hand. He was about to slip it back in its sheath and continue on his way when a voice startled him. His senses froze as he stiffened in the saddle.

"You no need the rifle."

Slocum twisted around to see who was speaking to him.

There, like an apparition, sat a man on a burro, a man whose skin was the color of red clay and whose face was hairless. He wore a red bandanna around his forehead and his hair was as white as snow, with long tresses that flowed to his shoulders.

"I am called Abeja. I come from the house of Carmen Delgado," he said. "I follow you from the town."

"You are the one who has been following me."

"And them," Abeja said, pointing toward a distant spot on the road."

Slocum saw two tiny dots on the horizon. Two riders, too far away for him to identify. They were riding slow, as if they were studying his tracks, sorting them out from all of the others on the road.

"I see them. Who are they?"

"They are of the sheriff. Jones and Smith."

"Well, I'll be damned."

"I rub out your tracks to this place," Abeja said. "They will not find us here."

"Hell, they can see us," Slocum said.

"We will go."

"Where?"

"I take you to Hidalgo."

The man was soft-spoken, but his voice had a deep timbre to it. His dark eyes glinted with something savage and wild.

"You are not Mexican," Slocum said.

"No. *Soy Indio. Indio puro.*"

"And you know Carmen Delgado."

"She is my goddaughter."

"But she is not Indian. Not pure Indian."

"No. She is mestiza. She has the white blood in her."

Slocum watched the two dots. They were riding in separate circles now, as if trying to find his tracks. Abeja had done a good job, he thought.

"Come," Abeja said. "We go to Hidalgo."

That was the place Carmen had mentioned, the settlement where she lived. Slocum followed Abeja as he turned his burro and crossed the creek, heading north and east across a rocky and desolate land filled with tumbleweeds and brush, creosote and mesquite. He felt he had to trust Abeja, for he was a stranger here and men were determined to either drive him out of town or kill him.

The sun sank lower in the west until its lower rim touched the horizon and then their shadows began to stretch across the trackless wasteland. A breeze sprang up and tumbleweeds rolled in every direction as aimless as Slocum felt now, although he was certain that Abeja knew exactly where they were.

As the sun dropped even lower, Slocum saw the whitewashed adobes glistening in the last rays of daylight and soon, they came to Hidalgo, a scattered jumble of humble huts, jacales and adobes that seemed to have been built with no pattern in mind. All the time they had ridden, Abeja had not said a word, but neither had he looked over his shoulder.

They entered the settlement and Slocum saw bony-ribbed dogs slinking here and there, scrawny cats furtively darting behind shacks and under little porches. Flowers in pots sat at every hovel, bright as fresh paint, adding color to a drab world that was now filling with shadows, the white adobe walls ghostly in the twilight.

Abeja reined his burro in front of a house that had a black wreath of woven vines on the door. It was very quiet. No children were playing and he had not seen a single soul who inhabited Hidalgo.

"This is the house of Carmen and her mother," Abeja said.

"Are we stopping here, then?"

"You will go in and then return. I will take you to a little house where you can stay."

"Why are you doing this, Abeja?"

"Carmen say to do this. The men who were following you, those men you saw, I think they wanted to kill you."

"Why do you think this?" Slocum asked.

"The Mexicans in town are like spirits. They are not seen by the whites. They are seen only as shadows, as pieces of wood, as rocks with no faces, no hearts."

"What do you mean?"

"They are invisible, the Mexicans. So they see much. They hear much. There is one who brings the food to the jail. He has big ears. He hear the sheriff tell those two who followed you to find you and make sure you do not come back to Del Rio."

"Did this man hear why they wanted me killed?"

"The sheriff, he say that a man will pay the money if you do not come back to town."

"What man? Did your friend hear a name?"

"Yes," Abeja said. "He hear the name of the man who will pay the money."

"And what is that name?" Slocum asked, almost fearful of hearing it.

"The man is called Rankins. Frank Rankins."

"Rankins? The banker?"

"That is the one."

Slocum swore under his breath.

So, he thought, Rankins knows what's at stake with the land. He's in on it, with Hardesty and Cordelia, and probably with the judge, the sheriff and Fernandez, the hangman. And his wife, Pandora. A conspiracy, wider than he had thought. But why let Hardesty buy the land?

Why not just kill him and let Rankins buy it for himself? Or Wyman? He wished he knew what the hell was going on.

"You go in now," Abeja said.

A curtain fluttered at a window. The door opened.

Slocum stepped out of the saddle. Abeja held out his hand to take the reins. Slocum handed them to him.

Carmen appeared in the doorway. She looked wan and tired.

"John," she said. "Come in. My brother is here."

She was dressed in black, a dark shawl over her jet hair. He heard a match strike as he walked toward her and a lamp came on inside the adobe hut, throwing Carmen into silhouette, a dark silhouette that seemed part of the night, an apparition not of this world at all.

She stepped back to allow Slocum to enter, and he walked inside to find a table in the center of the room on which lay a coffin. Next to it stood Carmen's mother, also garbed in black. She held a candle in her hand and was lighting another oil lamp. The room danced with shadows and, from another room, he heard a rustling and soft whispers, as if ghostly beings had gathered in this place of death, gathered in silence to mourn.

14

The whisperers emerged from the other room, two young girls and an older woman. Like Remedios, a rosary dangled from the older woman's hands. They were dressed in ordinary, simple clothing and stood silently in front of one wall, looking at Slocum as if he were a traveler from a distant land who had come to Hidalgo by mistake. Slocum took off his hat and nodded to the three women.

"John," Carmen said. "Abeja will take you to a little adobe, which is comfortable. He, or someone, will bring you food. I think it is very dangerous for you to stay in Del Rio. You will be safe here."

"Thank you, but it's not necessary," he said.

"I think it is necessary. I need you. Now, more than ever. Tomorrow, we will cook and have friends over to say good-bye to my brother. I would like you here. There will be whiskey and wine and good food and we will tell stories about Luis. There will be some grieving, but there will also be some laughter."

"I don't know. I'm not good at these things."

"Go with Abeja now. I will try and slip away later to visit you. We can talk more about it then. I have learned some things since I last saw you."

"Some things?"

"They may be important. For now, your life is in much danger. That is why I sent Abeja to find you, bring you to Hidalgo."

"You're very kind, Carmen."

"And you are a kind man, John Slocum. *Vaya con Dios.* My little bee will take you to a place where you can get some rest."

"Little bee?"

"Abeja. That is what his name means in Spanish. 'Bee.' "

He knew she was dismissing him and he did feel uncomfortable being in such a sad house. He nodded to Remedios, Carmen's mother, and she nodded back, unsmiling. He walked outside and heard the door close behind him.

Abeja handed Slocum the reins and Slocum mounted his horse. He followed the man down a long street, past dark adobes. They turned a corner and came upon another adobe sitting out in the open. In the gloaming, it looked abandoned, but he saw orange light spilling from under the door and around the windows.

"This is your little house, John Slocum," Abeja said. "Here you can stay for as long as you wish."

"Thank you."

"I will take your horse and unsaddle it. You take your bedding and rifle inside with you. I will give your horse some grain to make it strong for the next sun."

"Will you be the one to bring me food?" Slocum asked. "Carmen said that you might be."

"Yes."

"Then, will you have supper with me, Abeja? You seem a wise man who knows much, and I am a blind man in the darkness of Del Rio."

"It would be an honor, Slocum."

Slocum smiled, feeling good about the invitation. He felt he could learn from this quiet man who had led him out of danger. Del Rio was beginning to look like a town full of snakes and perhaps he could find out enough about the bad people to let him walk through it without getting bit.

Slocum swung down out of the saddle, removed his bedroll, with the sawed-off Greener wrapped inside it, his saddlebags and his Winchester. He handed the reins to Abeja, who took them.

When the Indio turned in the saddle, Slocum noticed that he not only wore a knife inside his waistband, but a piece of rope embraced his shoulder, and the rope held an old, sawed-off rifle that resembled a Sharps. The man's weapons were so well-concealed, Slocum hadn't noticed them either at the creek or on their ride to Hidalgo.

"You have a rifle," Slocum said.

"If a man owns a horse or burro and a gun, he is very rich," Abeja said.

"Why is the barrel sawed off?"

Abeja chuckled.

"A dying soldier used it to pry his wagon from the mud of the Rio Grande," Abeja said. "Many seasons ago. The barrel was bent from the middle to the nose. I found it and I cut off the crooked part. In the wagon, I found many *cartuchos*, the rifle cartridges. I have learned how to take out the lead bullet and load the cartridge with small stones or pieces of lead so that I can hunt the quail and the dove."

"A Sharps rifle?"

"I do not know what it is called. I cannot read the white man's words."

"It would not be accurate at long range," Slocum said.

"*Yo soy Indio*. I am Indian. I do not fight at the long range. It is the way of the coward."

"I will not ask you about the wagon and the soldiers," Slocum said. "It was a long time ago. And I was a soldier once."

"I know this. It was a long time ago. This place has been under many flags and we no longer count the killings of men or sing our songs of fighting and bravery. The old ways are gone and we live like the weeds that grow from the ground even when there is no water and the sun is very hot."

Slocum hefted his saddlebags and turned toward the adobe.

"I look forward to talking to you when we have supper," he said.

"I will bring the wine with the *comida*," Abeja said. "It will make the talk easy to do."

Slocum smiled and walked to the door. He opened it. When he turned around, Abeja was gone and he heard only the whisper of Ferro's hooves in the darkness.

There was a single oil lamp burning on a small, handmade table. There was a mat on the floor for sleeping, another larger table next to the wall and three chairs that seemed to have been salvaged from some cast-off dump site. In another room, there was a fire ring and a pit, over which hung a metal rod set on forked metal stakes where people had once cooked. The place smelled musty and he saw a rat scurry along the wall and then disappear through a hole that led outside. There were cobwebs, old ones, in two of the corners of the cooking room, their white strands glazed with a copper glow from the lamp in the front room.

Slocum set down his saddlebags and rifle, then unwrapped his bedroll and laid it atop the sleeping mat. He noticed little niches cut into the adobe brick walls and, in one of them, was a crumbling statue to some saint, the colors faded, the features blurred.

He sat on one of the chairs and it was sturdy enough to hold his weight. He reached into a saddlebag on the floor and pulled out a bottle of Kentucky bourbon wrapped in a towel. He uncorked it and set it on the table. He removed his frock coat and took a cheroot from an inside pocket. He struck a match and lit it, then took a swallow of the whiskey. The warm liquid flowed down his throat and into his belly. He smoked and felt good that he was in this peaceful place where he could think and use reason to figure out his next move.

Greed, Slocum thought, was like a strong itch. Once a greedy person smelled money, or wealth, he would stop at nothing to obtain it. No obstacle was too great, including murder. From what he had been able to glean from the events surrounding his short stay in Del Rio, not only was there strong evidence that Bill Hardesty wanted the one hundred thousand acres, on which gold was supposedly hidden, but that he had gone through an elaborate scheme to obtain the property. Or had he? A woman had killed Granby and framed an innocent man for her crime. But was she in cahoots with Hardesty? And where did Judge Wyman fit in? Was he also a cohort of Hardesty's? Which led Slocum to think of Fernandez, the hangman. And his wife. She obviously enjoyed the grisly spectacle of seeing a man's neck breaking at the end of a rope.

But if the hanging of Luis Delgado was to cover up a conspiracy, who orchestrated the entire scheme? If the banker, Rankins, had been in on it, he could have just refused to loan Granby enough money to buy the property in question. However, Slocum had learned that Hardesty had been turned down for a loan on the same piece of land. Why, then, with the murder of Granby, was Hardesty probably going to get a loan? Had he been forced to reveal that there was a fortune in gold buried somewhere on that huge acreage? If so, then he would have had to cut in Rankins, and he had probably had to offer shares to the sheriff, his deputies, perhaps, and the hangman, along with the hangman's lady, Pandora.

Slocum took another small swig of whiskey and shook his head. It was all too complicated to figure out in his present state of weariness. There were too many people involved for him to sort it all out just then. But he kept coming back to Luis Delgado.

Why had he been chosen to hang for the murder of Granby? Out of all the people in Del Rio, why Delgado? And who had been the woman who danced with him and fired the killing shot? He would have to get to the bottom of that. And somewhere in the mix was the bailiff, Rufus Early. He had been the one to contact Delgado and take him to the hotel. So Early was in on the scheme as well. Judge Wyman's bailiff.

And finally, Slocum wondered who the two men had been who came to murder him in his hotel room. Did Hardesty know about that? If so, why had he brought his daughter, Lorelei, to town? If Lorelei had been in his room when the killers came, she would have been dead, too. Was Hardesty that cold-blooded? Would he stop at nothing to achieve his goal of wealth? It was hard to imagine a man who would kill his own daughter, but it was not beyond all reason.

The more he thought of those things, all the loose ends, the more puzzling everything became for Slocum. What he should do, he knew, deep in his heart, was to ride out the next morning and leave Del Rio behind. Forget about Delgado and Hardesty, Wyman and Fernandez and all the little soldiers carrying spears in this complex Greek tragedy.

But he wouldn't do that. He had an itch, too. Not for wealth, but for knowledge.

Somehow, he knew, he had to find out who the woman

was who had murdered Granby. And he had to find out why Wyman and Fernandez would conspire to murder innocent men in public.

In Slocum's experience, this puzzle seemed to point one way. In most men's affairs, in war and in peace, there was always a common denominator behind what men did to each other. It could be summed up by an old French saying that he had read in a dime detective novel: *Cherchez la femme*.

"Look for the woman."

Somewhere, Slocum thought, behind the murder of Granby, the hanging of Delgado, the attempts on his own life, there was a woman.

He had neglected to focus on Granby's wife. She was now with Hardesty as if that had been prearranged. If so, why? But she had not shot her husband. She had been a witness. A lying witness, no doubt.

No, there was another woman behind all of this and Slocum had a strong hunch where to look for her. In a way, she was the most enigmatic of all the people involved in the hangings, murder, deceit and betrayal.

One woman.

A woman with the cold heart of a killer.

And that was the woman he must find.

15

Abeja returned with a large wicker basket of hot food for his and Slocum's supper. They sat down to a meal of spiced beef strips, steaming tortillas, refried beans and rice, which they washed down with a sturdy red wine. The two men spoke little during the meal, but afterward, outside, Abeja accepted a cheroot from Slocum. The two men leaned against the adobe wall in the darkness, looking up at the tapestry of bright stars spread across the heavens.

"You will see the banker tomorrow," Abeja said.

"If I can. But I don't think he will be of much help."

"You want to know why Luis Delgado was made to look like a murderer."

"I think I know why, Abeja. I just don't know who planned it. I think there is a woman behind it. After all, it was a woman who shot and killed the rancher, Granby."

"I think you know how to track the fox," Abeja said. "Who is the woman?"

"I don't know. Wish I did. Someone very cool and calculating. Do you understand what I mean?"

"A cat," Abeja said, his deep voice soft like a dry corn

husk stirred by a gentle breeze. "Very patient, eh? Very sure."

"Yes. The woman danced as if she had not a care in the world and then she shot a man in cold blood."

"Then you will know who to look for, Slocum."

"I'm not sure. I don't know where to start."

Abeja drew on the cheroot and smacked his lips as he let the smoke back out of his lungs. The smoke rose in the air over his head like a thin scrim over the sky. The stars twinkled like the distant lights of a town.

"The wolf can wear the hide of an antelope," Abeja said. "The antelope will think the wolf is of their tribe. Until the wolf wants to eat one of them. Then the wolf gives himself away. When he opens his mouth to bite, he becomes a wolf again and the antelope hide falls off."

"Like a leopard cannot change its spots," Slocum said.

"Is this how you say it in English? One is who he is. A thing is what it is. The wolf cannot be the antelope. The spotted leopard cannot paint its spots."

"Yes. Like a man's habit. Or a woman's."

"Follow the tracks," Abeja said. "Always follow the tracks. These, too, do not change."

Abeja left a short while later and Slocum went inside. There was no latch on the door, so he could not lock it. This did not bother him. He was a light sleeper and always kept one eye open when he was sleeping under the stars or in a strange bed.

As he lay there on his bedroll atop the sleeping mat, he thought of Carmen, wondered how she was handling her grief. Her house was probably filled with women helping her to get through it. But it was a sad time and his own heart was filled with a kind of sadness that had as much to do with justice as it did with Delgado's wrongful death. An innocent man had died. Why? Because of another man's greed.

He had run into greed after the war when he returned home to find crooked judges and carpetbaggers gobbling up all the land for next to nothing. People taking advantage of others, less fortunate. Yes, the South had lost the war, but they were still Americans, and the men had been off fighting for what they believed was a just cause, the right to choose their own destiny, without interference from the government. Life, liberty and the pursuit of happiness; all guaranteed by the United States Constitution. But that was not what Slocum had found back in Calhoun County, Georgia.

Drowsiness overtook him and Slocum dropped off a dark precipice and into a deep sleep. He had been more tired than he had thought, he supposed, and he found himself swimming deep in dream, oblivious to all danger, all outside cares of the waking world.

Slocum turned over in his sleep and that might have saved his life. He heard a thud from somewhere far off in the dream, and through the cotton of his ears, rough, gruff voices, whispering. Instantly, he was awake and scrambling to get away from hands that were reaching for him, grasping his neck as if to choke him into senselessness or death.

"You son of a bitch," a gravely voice intoned, "you were told to get your ass out of town."

"Get him. He's gettin' away," another voice growled.

Slocum heard scuffling noises and tried to adjust his eyes to the darkness of the room. It was pitch-black and he could not make out any definition of objects.

"Where is he?"

"He ain't down there, Smitty."

Suddenly, Slocum knew who his attackers were. The two deputies, Smitty and Jones. He lashed out at the last voice he heard, Jones's, and felt his fist strike cloth, a soft mass, like a shoulder.

"Ow," Jones whispered in a loud voice. "The bastard."

Then one of them, probably Smitty, drove a fist into Slocum's gut. He felt the air rush out of his lungs and he doubled over in pain. He heard a hissing sound over his head and knew that Jones had taken a swipe at him.

"Slocum, you can make it easy on yourself," Smitty said. "We just mean to give you a drubbing and run you out of town. Don't make us kill you."

Slocum drew back and loosed a straight shot at the sound of the voice. His knuckles smashed into something hard that went soft as mush. He felt a warm rush of blood drenching his knuckles and knew he had probably broken a nose.

Slocum circled his invisible attackers, pushing away from the wall, sliding along another until he ran into the edge of the big table. He heard one of the men crash into a chair and send it skidding across the floor in a screech of wood. He waded out into the center of the room, away from the table where he would have been trapped and bowled into a body. He rammed a right and a left into the man's midsection and side, heard him grunt and expel air from his lungs. He sidestepped and ducked a haymaker, then rammed an uppercut into the man's chin, knocking him backward into the table.

The other man, Smitty, he thought, came at him then, wielding a pistol, Slocum believed, and slashed at him with the butt, just grazing his arm and bouncing off his shoulder. Slocum kicked at the man, aiming for the groin. He hit a leg, the upper thigh and the man grunted in pain.

"Get him, Jonesy," Smith snarled. "Knee him in the nuts."

Slocum felt hands grab at him, grasping his shoulders. He doubled over and spun away as Jones rammed a knee toward Slocum's groin. Slocum felt a fist slam into the side of his face, mashing his left cheek. A starburst of lights exploded in his head and he reeled from the solid blow. The two men closed in on him and fists slammed into his sides and solar plexus. He groaned in pain, knowing he would go down if he didn't escape their pincer movement.

Darker shapes moved in front and around Slocum, as if his eyes were becoming adjusted to the darkness. He warded off fists and kicking boots, swaying from side to side to avoid the blows that sailed out of inky blackness into forms that danced before his eyes like black blobs. But he knew he was outnumbered and the deputies could see better than he, for they had come through the night and their eyes had adjusted.

Slocum lowered his head and charged between the two men, his fists flailing at the end of his windmilling arms. He smacked flesh on their faces and felt them move away under the impact of his balled up fists. But then they grabbed at him and snatched at his clothing, holding him back. A fist hammered into the small of his back and he felt pain surge through him. He spun around again and started looking for a way out. Where was the door? No light seeped through the opening in the adobe and he knew the door was closed, locking out starlight and moonlight.

They were on him like pouncing cats, pummeling him with hammer-hard fists. He felt blood streaking from a fissure in his check as a fist broke the skin. A fist slammed into his right eye and blinded him with pain. The eye began to swell and the darkness around him grew as tears flowed from the swollen eye.

Now, it was all pain and Slocum felt his resistance ebbing. He rammed an elbow into one of the men, but that only made him a better target. He grappled with the other man and felt the weight of him on his arms, pushing him downward. Then his legs turned to rubber and jelly as a flurry of fists drove into his belly and chest, seemingly from all directions.

"You're goin' down, you bastard," Jones rasped and Slocum felt a fist smash into his jaw. More lights danced in his head and then his knees bent and gave way. He slumped down under the rain of blows and one of the men rammed a knee into his face, breaking the skin, smashing veins and capillaries and knocking him senseless.

Then the door burst open and he heard a voice he recognized.

"Let's light a shuck. Finish him off."

Slocum barely saw Rufus Early's silhouette in the open doorway.

One of the men stepped up to him and smashed him with the butt of his pistol, hammering straight down on the top of Slocum's head and the dancing lights blurred and vanished as he sank into a Stygian pit where there was no light, no sense, no anything but oblivion.

Somewhere in the distance he heard footsteps and the scrapings of boots and then all sound faded. He fought to rise out of the well of blackness, but all thought was jumbled, askew, useless and he lay there panting in his deafness, his lungs burning, his body screaming in pain. One of the men had kicked him before bolting out the door and Slocum felt the agony of it in his side as if his body had caved in and there was a bruise there, spreading like a blazing stain.

Slocum sank into unconsciousness, shackled in the irons of pain like some battered prisoner chained to a dank dungeon wall.

The bare beginnings of feeble sunlight streamed through the open door of the adobe. Slocum awoke to groans somewhere outside. His head throbbed with a pulsating pain and his body seemed to be one huge bruise from the top of his head to his ankles. He struggled to his knees, feeling knives in his ribs where one of the attackers had kicked him. He steeled himself and rose to his feet. He stood on wobbly legs, struggling to get his bearings through a fuzz of thoughts that seemed all tangled up like frayed yarn.

"Slocum," a voice called from outside. The voice was weak and raspy, but Slocum recognized it as belonging to Abeja. "Slocum."

"Give me a minute," Slocum said, forcing his voice through a throat sore from the pounding he had taken. Blood caked the side of his face and his ears rang like church bells on Sunday morning.

He wobbled to the door, every step bringing pain that shot through his body like hot lances, or knifed his torso with stinging daggers.

Abeja lay outside, bound with manila rope, his hands and feet tied tightly, the rope knotted several times. The sun was not yet up over the horizon, but there was plenty of light now, light that spread to the shadows of a sleeping village, its inhabitants seemingly unaware of the fight that had occurred in their midst sometime in the early morning hours.

Slocum untied Abeja and watched as he stretched his arms and legs, rubbed his wrists to restore the circulation of blood to his fingers and hands.

"They jumped me," he said. "They knocked me cold. I just woke up." He looked up at Slocum. "You look like they got you, too."

"They found us," Slocum said.

"They did not kill you."

"No, and I'm not sure why. They were trying to run me out of town, I guess."

"And will you now go away?"

Abeja got to his feet. He stood there with his feet wide

apart, as if for balance, and shaded his eyes from the rising sun.

"No, Abeja. Those boys chalked up a big debt with me. There were two of them who worked me over, Smitty and Jones. But the bailiff, Early, was outside, I guess to keep anyone from coming in or to watch over you."

"What will you do, Slocum?"

"If they come at me again, I will kill them," Slocum said, and his jaw, despite the pain, hardened until a muscle twitched like some warning nerve, the same way a cat's tail quivers just before it makes its kill.

16

Carmen tied the last of the tightly wound strips of cloth she had used as a bandage around Slocum's rib cage and sat back to survey her work. She had put some kind of a mixture on his chest and side that was cool and soothing.

"I do not think they broke any of your ribs," she said. "But you must be sore all over. Poor Abeja. He never complains, but he has a knot on his head as big as a duck egg."

"Abeja and I were both lucky," Slocum said.

Slocum and Abeja had walked, painfully, over to Carmen's house after drenching themselves with water from the town well, and she had prepared breakfast for them, then tended to their wounds.

"In Del Rio, if you stay, John, your luck may turn bad."

"I have to get to the bottom of this conspiracy, Carmen. I am going into town today to ask some questions. I will not be here for your brother's wake. But I will pay my respects this morning, before I go. I am sorry for your loss."

"I do not know what my mother and I will do," she

said. "With my brother gone, we will have no way to earn money. He was our support."

"What did your brother do?" Slocum asked.

"He worked for Mr. Hardesty on his ranch," she said.

Slocum reared back in his chair.

"What?"

"I said that Luis worked for Mr. Bill Hardesty. That is why I was surprised that he did not say some good things about my brother at the trial."

"Do you know what your brother did for Hardesty?"

"He worked the cattle. He was a vaquero. But for the last month, he told us that he was digging in the ground on some land."

"Digging? Where?"

"On some land Mr. Hardesty wanted to buy."

"Did he tell you if he found anything?"

"Just before . . ." Carmen choked up and tried to keep from breaking down and crying. She sniffed and dabbed at her eyes with a handkerchief, then continued. "Maybe a day or two before . . . you know . . . he said his shovel struck some metal and some wood. Mr. Hardesty was there. He said that Mr. Hardesty sent him back to the rancho."

"So, your brother never did find out what was in the ground?"

"No. He said it looked like a chest. It was made of wood and had metal straps on it."

"Do you know if any other men who worked for Hardesty were ever hanged?"

A look came over Carmen's face, as if someone had wiped it with a hot cloth. Her eyes glittered and her lips tightened in a grimace.

"Let me think," she said.

Slocum waited.

Finally, Carmen drew in a deep breath, then let it out.

"That's funny," she said, "because my brother mentioned that when he first started to work for Mr. Hardesty . . ."

"What?"

"Luis said that it was a . . . a . . . , oh, what is the English word? Like a bad thing, maybe, to work on the Rocking H."

"A jinx?"

"Yes," she said. "The jinx. He said that two other young men he knew, Pablo Cardoza and Rafael Fuentes, had been caught stealing cows and the judge had hanged them. I did not think anything of this at the time."

"Anyone else?" Slocum asked.

She shook her head.

"I do not know. Those are the only two I can think of. We did not believe either Pablo or Rafael had stolen any cattle. They were honest men."

"I'm sure," Slocum said, his mind racing.

He knew he had to find out more. But a pattern was emerging, and it was ugly. And diabolical. It began to look like Luis Delgado wasn't just a random pick for a setup, but that there was a purpose behind his execution that, in a sense, killed two birds with one stone. If Hardesty had wanted to shut him up because Delgado had found one of the strongboxes containing gold, and if he had wanted to eliminate Granby as the buyer of the valuable property, then the job had been pulled off very neatly. Almost.

"I'm going into Del Rio," Slocum said, after a few moments. "There are things I have to find out, things I need to know."

"You should not go there," she said.

"I have to, Carmen."

"Oh, John, I have fear that I will never see you again. Will you come back here and stay in the little adboe? We will put guards up so that you can sleep safe the next time."

"I will come back," he promised her.

Slocum got up and walked into the next room where the body of Luis Delgado lay in the open casket. There were women seated all around the room, some squatting on the floor, some in chairs, others on wooden boxes. They were all saying their beads.

"They are saying a novena for my brother," Carmen explained.

Slocum stood before the casket and looked down at the waxen brown face of the dead man. He took off his hat and murmured a short prayer.

"I will get justice for you, Luis," he said softly. "*Vaya con Dios.*"

"Thank you, John. I know God will hear your prayer."

"Good-bye, Carmen. Tell Abeja thanks for me. Tell him not to follow me to town."

"I will tell him," she said.

Abeja had Slocum's horse saddled and waiting for him outside the adobe where he had spent the night. The Indian's burro was there, too.

"You go to Del Rio?" Abeja said.

"Yes, but you must stay here."

"I have a gun. I have a knife. You will be, how do you say it, out of numbers?"

"Outnumbered," Slocum said.

"Yes, outnumbered. Too many guns in Del Rio. Too many bad men."

"Look. Sit tight. I'm going to stay here in Hidalgo. Make it my headquarters. I'll be back this afternoon or tonight."

"*Ten cuidado,*" Abeja said.

Slocum rode away from Hidalgo. He knew what Abeja

SLOCUM AND THE HANGMAN'S LADY 123

had said to him in Spanish. "Be careful." "Take care." He would do that, he promised himself.

He formed a plan in his mind that would help him find the answers he needed. He knew that once he began asking questions, the danger to him would increase. And it would all boil down to a simple matter. Whom could he trust? Surely, he thought, there must be a few honest men in Del Rio. But how much were they willing to risk when he started digging for the truth?

Slocum left Ferro at the stables and walked first to the Land Office, where he enquired about the ownership of the one hundred thousand acres. A Mr. Huckabee gave him the information, including directions to the house of the owner.

"She's a widder woman, livin' in that big old house over on Oak Street," Huckabee said. "She don't get out much."

Slocum knocked on the door of the house owned by Mrs. Wilbur Loomis. The land clerk had said her first name was Belinda. A Mexican woman opened the door.

"Mrs. Loomis," Slocum said. "Is she in?"

"She is in the front room. Follow me."

Slocum followed the maid through the foyer and into the front room. An old woman sat in a rocking chair, a blanket over her lap, touching the carpeted floor. She looked up, her eyes rheumy from age, her tousled gray hair framing her small oval face.

"A man to see you, Belinda," the maid said and left the room.

"Sit down," Belinda said. "My, you are a tall drink of water, feller. What brings you to my humble home? Do you want to buy my land? It's got a curse on it, you know."

Slocum wondered if Belinda Loomis was addled. He

sat down in a straight-backed chair with a cushioned seat and backing.

"Scoot up close," she said. "My old eyes don't see too good anymore."

"Yes'm."

"What's your name, son?"

Slocum told her.

"You from around here?"

"No'm. I'm just wondering about that land you're selling."

"Mr. Rankins send you?"

"In a way."

"He told me he was selling the land to a man named Grady or Grabby, or something like that."

"Mr. Granby died," Slocum said.

"Oh my. He did? What a shame. It's the curse, I reckon."

"Yes'm. Can you tell me about the curse?"

"No, I can't. It's a mystery. My husband, rest his soul, was not the first to die, but he was the first to hang. Since then, there's been many others. All of 'em hanged, or shot."

"I don't understand. What happened to your husband? Why was he hanged?"

Belinda sighed and lifted the shawl that draped her frail shoulders. In her hand was a small glass filled with amber-colored liquid. She took a sip and the whiskey fumes floated to Slocum's nostrils. She smacked her lips as her eyes filled with tears. She gave a small cough and then opened her mouth. Her lips started moving, but no sound came out at first. She looked like a fish gasping for oxygen.

"Poor Wilbur," she said, her voice suddenly issuing from her scalded throat. "The law said he rustled cattle. They found some Rocking H whitefaces on our property and they took him off. Judge Wyman tried him for rustling and Carlos Fernandez hanged him. Lordy, I never cried so much in my life. I knew Wilbur never stole no cattle. He didn't even like cattle. He inherited that land from his pappy and wanted to grow tomaters and squash and taters on it."

"And since then?" Slocum said. "Others have died, you say?"

"Oh, a heap of folks," she said. "That land is cursed. I know it."

From Belinda, Slocum learned that others had tried to buy the land or worked on it and all of them had died of unnatural causes.

"Did you know there was gold buried on your property?" Slocum asked, as Belinda took another sip of her whiskey. He figured she would be drunk by the time her glass was empty.

"Oh, there've been rumors about that for a long while now. The Mexicans say the Spaniards buried gold there and others say bandits came across the border and buried gold all over. There's no gold there. Just blood. Lots of blood."

"Thank you, Mrs. Loomis. I'll leave you now."

"Just what was it you wanted, Mr. Slocum?"

"Just information."

"You go to the newspaper. They'll tell you the names of all those who died over that accursed land. They gave me a list once and asked me to make a statement. I told them it would do no good. I'd like to sell the land, though. I need the money and there's no one to tend to it."

"Yes'm." Slocum got up and put the chair back where it had been. "Thank you."

"I like you, Mr. Slocum. You go see Mr. Rankins about buying that land. Maybe you can take the curse off'n it."

She saluted Slocum with her glass and downed the rest

of it. Her eyes turned even more bleary and she sank back into her shawl and blanket, a small wizened figure of a woman who had probably been beautiful once. Now, she was a living skeleton who believed in curses and mourned, still, the death of her husband.

The Mexican maid let Slocum out.

"She is dying, you know," the maid said. "She is killing herself every day."

"Yes," Slocum said. "I know. It seems to be going around here in Del Rio."

The maid looked at him dumbly and Slocum touched a finger to his hat and walked across the porch and down the steps.

He felt as if he had just visited a funeral parlor.

17

The publisher of the newspaper, the *Del Rio Times*, was reluctant to talk to Slocum, at first.

"You say Belinda Loomis sent you over here?" Vernon Cunningham said. He sat like a giant toad on a mushroom, his head wreathed in blue cigar smoke, his pudgy lips almost obscene with saliva. His desk, a large one, seemed small next to Cunningham's bulk. His bald head glistened with sweat and from the sunlight streaming through the window behind his desk. The desk was strewn with papers, even though there was a two-tiered wooden box that read IN and OUT. These, too, were crammed full of scrawled copy.

"She suggested I talk to you, Mr. Cunningham. She said you kept a list of those who have been hanged in the past several months. Or years."

"I know who you are, Slocum. You were a witness in that Delgado mockery of a trial."

"I believe, in fact I know, that Luis Delgado was innocent."

"Slocum, you're a marked man. Those look like fresh bruises on your face. Somebody work you over?"

"A couple of deputies."

"Jones and Smith, likely. They're thugs. Wonder they didn't kill you, but they usually stop short of that, far as I can see."

"They wanted me to run."

"But you didn't."

"Cunningham, there's something rotten here in Del Rio. You know it and I know it. Does it all go back to Judge Wyman?"

"He's got a hand in it, certainly. I think someone pays him off. To be unjudiciously judicious, if you know what I mean."

"Do you know who that might be?" Slocum asked.

"I have a strong hunch."

"Hardesty?"

"Ah, you spoke the magic word. Nothing provable, of course. But all roads lead to Rome, they say."

"Are you saying you've looked into the hangings and found a connection between them and Bill Hardesty?"

Cunningham spun around in his swivel chair. He looked out the window. He swung back and wore a frown on his face.

"Look, Slocum, I don't know some of the things that go on in this town any more than you do, but my hands are tied. The last newspaper guy who tried to print the truth, or speculate, wound up dead, his office burned."

"So you, like everybody else in Del Rio, are running scared."

"I've got a lot of stuff stored away, in a safe place, and I intend to, one day, get a congressman, or a lawmaker up in Austin, to take a look at it. But I don't have much proof. Those men Wyman hanged were all given trials and convicted and he meted out the proper punishment. According to the law. Never mind that the evidence against those men was weak or faulty. In Texas, like everywhere else, the law is the law, and the judge is king of the dadblamed hill."

"I have a list of names," Slocum said. "All hanged by Judge Wyman. All of them had something to do with some land west of town, where supposedly gold is buried."

"Supposedly. Yeah, I know the land, owned by Mrs. Loomis. It's crazy. I've never seen any gold that was found there. Rumors. That's all it is."

"What if it isn't?" Slocum asked.

"Then there's blood on it. I know Hardesty wants that land. Tried to buy it. Rankins turned him down."

"But now Hardesty seems to have taken Granby's wife under his wing and he's going to buy the land. Rankins is going to loan him the money."

Cunningham let out a low whistle.

"That's worth looking into. I know Granby was set to get a loan when he was killed."

"Who do you think killed him?" Slocum asked.

"I have no idea. You said you saw a woman shoot him."

"I'm looking for that woman. Any ideas?"

Cunningham shrugged.

"Nope. None. We never had a woman up on murder charges here in Del Rio before."

"I have a hunch who that woman is," Slocum said.

There was a silence in the room. Cunningham stared at Slocum as if he suspected Slocum might have lost his senses. He puffed on his cigar and spewed out smoke like some potbellied volcano getting ready to erupt.

"If it's slander I can't print it," Cunningham said. "If it's libel, I can't print it. And if it's anybody prominent, even if I have proof, I can't print it."

"Why?"

"I don't want to lose either my life or my newspaper."

"All right, I'll keep my hunch to myself for a time."

"Might be best. And what might be even better would be for you to forget all about Del Rio and Luis Delgado and just go on back to wherever you came from. Well, let me correct that. I know you can't go back to Georgia. Sheriff Curt Blandings has already been here with information that leads me to believe you're still wanted for murder back in Calhoun County."

"Word gets around," Slocum said.

"It sure as hell does."

Slocum could see that he was going to get nowhere with Cunningham. But he already knew that the publisher had a file on the hangings and was hoping one day to go outside Del Rio and ask for a full investigation. That could take months, if not years, when Cunningham decided he had enough evidence to seek help in Austin or Washington, D.C. By that time, all of the criminals would have covered their tracks. It would take years more to find out the truth about the hangings, the hidden gold and the conspiracy involving Bill Hardesty, who seemed to be at the center pole of every lead Slocum was following.

"Maybe I'll see you another time, Slocum," Cunningham said, putting his cigar out in a huge bowl he used for an ashtray. Maybe I should have your obituary written up, just in case."

"What would you say about me?" Slocum asked.

"First off, I'd say you were a damned fool."

Slocum smiled.

"Be sure to put in the next line, if you do," Slocum said.

"And what line would that be, Mr. John Slocum?"

"Fools rush in where angels fear to tread, Mr. Cunningham."

"Touché."

Slocum walked to the Del Rio Bank, which was on

Main Street. He didn't expect to find out much from Rankins, but he had to talk to him. Sometimes a man gave himself away by what he didn't say. Slocum could often read a man by the look in his eyes or the way he moved his hands and his body.

"May I help you, sir?"

Slocum stood in front of a desk, looking around the bank lobby, which was not very large.

"I'd like to see Frank Rankins."

"Do you have an appointment, sir?"

"No, I don't," Slocum said.

"What's your name and what business do you have with Mr. Rankins?"

"John Slocum. Land."

"Buying land, are you?"

"Just give him my name," Slocum said.

The clerk got up from his desk and walked through a gate in a wooden railing. He entered a back office with Rankins's name on the door, signifying he was the president. In a few moments, the man returned.

"Mr. Rankins will see you for five minutes only. He has a previous appointment."

Slocum thanked the clerk and walked back to the office and opened the door.

Seated at a large oak desk was the man he had last seen in the Del Rio Hotel two nights before. He was dressed in a business suit and now wore spectacles that were horn-rimmed, gave him the look of an owl.

"Mr. Slocum, have a chair," Rankins said. "What brings you to my office? I thought you would have left town by now."

"Nope. Still here," Slocum said. He sat down, crossed his legs as if he meant to stay there awhile. Rankins frowned.

"And you have business with me?"

"Maybe. I understand you're going to loan Bill Hardesty money to buy the land owned by Mrs. Wilber Loomis. Belinda."

"I don't divulge private business matters, Mr. Slocum."

"I just wondered what changed your mind. You turned him down for a loan before. Before you planned to loan Granby the money he needed to buy that one hundred thousand acres."

"Sir, this is simply none of your business. Details of our loans to individuals or businesses are strictly private."

"Do you know who that woman was who danced with Luis Delgado the night Granby was killed? You were right there."

"Mr. Slocum, this meeting is over. Will you kindly leave?"

"Not until you answer my question." Slocum uncrossed his legs and flipped open his frock coat revealing the Colt .45 on his hip, the gun belt rowed with shiny brass cartridges.

Rankins swallowed something in his throat. His face turned pale as paste.

"No, I do not know who the woman was. I wasn't paying attention to those on the dance floor. I was conducting business with the Granbys. Now, please leave."

Slocum got up and walked to the front of Rankins's desk.

"I feel sorry for you, Mr. Rankins. You're a little turd floating on top of a cesspool, and you haven't got the balls to swim out of it."

"Sir," Rankins snapped, but he scooted his chair back a few inches to put distance between him and Slocum. His face was now red as a boiled beet.

Slocum turned and walked out, slamming the door behind him.

"Sir, did you find your meeting with Mr. Rankins satisfactory?" the clerk asked.

"Yes, I did. He's a mealy-mouthed son of a bitch, but quite pleasant."

Slocum smiled as the clerk gaped, his jaw dropping like a window sash.

Slocum left the bank and headed for the stables, watching the street on both sides. It wasn't until he reached the stables that he knew something was wrong.

Ferro was still saddled and tied to a hitching post outside of the barn. Slocum's rifle wasn't in its boot.

Slocum stopped and then circled the livery, coming up on the side where the two doors stood wide open.

Ferro whickered when he saw Slocum. He pawed the ground with his right foot.

Slocum listened for any sound. It was very quiet, and he knew that wasn't natural.

Then he heard something inside the stables. It was a small sound. A boot scraping on straw, the creak of leather, perhaps.

He waited. Listened.

Someone inside the barn cleared his throat.

Slocum drew his pistol, hearing the metal whisper against the leather. He put his thumb on the hammer of the single-action Colt.

It seemed an eternity before anything happened.

And then all hell broke loose.

18

Slocum whirled when he heard two hammers cocking. He went into a fighting crouch, thumbed back the hammer of his Colt. The man had sneaked up behind him and was bringing a double-barreled shotgun to his shoulder.

Slocum pointed the snout of his .45 at the man's midsection and squeezed the trigger. The pistol bucked in his hand. Once, twice.

The first bullet struck the man in the belt buckle, doubling him over. The second caught him in the throat. Blood spewed from the throat wound. The man's fingers tightened on the twin triggers as the shotgun pointed skyward. Both barrels blasted off, sending double ought buckshot straight up in the air. The man hit the ground, twitched and kicked, then lay still, blood gushing from his throat and back.

Then another man emerged from the barn. He, too, had a shotgun in his hands. When he saw Slocum spin back around to face him, a smoking pistol in his hand, the man started turning to go back into the livery. Slocum snapped off a shot at him. The bullet plowed a furrow in the ground where the man had been and sent up a cloud of dust.

Slocum walked back to the man he had just shot. He stuck a boot under his torso and turned him over for a better look. Deputy Smith was as dead as a stone, a grisly smile on his face, his eyes glassy and lifeless, staring up at a sun that no longer burned his retinas.

He walked back to the barn and sidled alongside the outer wall until he was near the entrance.

"Jones," Slocum called in, "Smitty's dead. If you want to join him in Boot Hill, just stay right where you are. If you don't, throw your shotgun out here and light a shuck."

There was no answer. Slocum waited, ejecting the two empty cartridges from his pistol and sliding two more full ones into the cylinder. He took the hammer off of half-cock and squatted down to present less of a target in case Deputy Jones decided to come after him and take his chances.

"All right," Jones called out. "I'm givin' up the shotgun, Slocum."

"Toss it out."

He heard a shuffling of feet, then a noise like a wind through a chimney. The shotgun came sailing out of the livery, *whoop, whoop, whoop*. It struck the ground and skidded to a stop. Slocum heard the sound of a man running. The footfalls stopped somewhere at the far end of the barn. Then he heard hoofbeats. Slocum wasted no time. He walked over to Ferro and untied him. He led the horse inside the livery, scanning every inch of the ground and wall.

He found what he was looking for. His Winchester was leaning against the wall, near the left corner. He picked it up and checked to see if it was still loaded. He pulled the lever and saw the brass gleam of a cartridge in the chamber. He closed the receiver and slid the rifle back in its boot. Then he mounted the horse and rode out the back of the stable. He saw Jones loping away, his vest flapping loosely on his back.

The deputy had wisely chosen to keep on breathing.

Slocum did not chase after him because he knew he could not linger in Del Rio. He still had one more place he wanted to go before returning to Hidalgo, but it was not in town. He put the spurs to Ferro and made a wide circle in the opposite direction of the fleeing Jones, crossing the creek and heading west toward the Rocking H, Hardesty's spread.

Slocum crossed and recrossed the creek, trying to hide his tracks. He knew he would be followed, perhaps not right away, but soon. Today, tomorrow. He had killed a sheriff's deputy and now they would be hunting him. And if they found him, they would shoot to kill. No questions asked. No hangman for him. Maybe, he thought, he should have killed Jones, too. Killed both of them.

He sighed as he neared the confluence of the Rio Grande and San Felipe Creek. It didn't matter. He would probably get another chance at Jones, and perhaps the sheriff himself, and those he brought with him to hunt him down.

Slocum rode toward the entrance to the Rocking H. He was in the open now, and he was wary. Del Rio wasn't the only dangerous place for him. He knew enough about Hardesty now to know that he was a man who would stop at nothing to achieve his aims. He may not have pulled the trigger on anyone, but he had most certainly killed men. That made him as dangerous as any gunslinger— more dangerous perhaps. He was a snake with no rattles. He could strike from anywhere and the victim would never know that Hardesty was the one with the venom.

Slocum rode to the fence line of Hardesty's ranch, the easternmost corner, where the creek formed a natural boundary. He rode into a grove of trees: cottonwood and

water oaks growing thick on both banks. There, he rested
Ferro and surveyed that corner of the Rocking H.

There were a few cattle grazing and doves sitting on
the top rail. Well inside, about a quarter mile away, a
stand of mesquite grew thick and he could see that men
had been working on cutting down the remaining trees
and bushes. It was too bad, Slocum thought. The mesquite
provided good cover for doves and quail, but he knew
cattlemen in south Texas hated the mesquite since it grew
so fast. The cattle would eat the leaves and berries and
then when they roamed, they dropped the seeds, which
did not digest, atop the pile of cowshit. This acted as a
fertilizer to the beans and where one grew, others
sprouted, spreading the thick tough brush in every direction.

As Slocum gazed at the ranchland, movement caught
his eye. Then he saw a familiar sight, a flash of white in
the mesquite grove, then a beautiful horse galloped into
view. It was Aladdin, under saddle, and someone was riding him, heading straight for him. As the rider drew
closer, Slocum's heart began to pound faster. He recognized the rider, too.

"John," Lorelei cried. "Wait for me."

He spurred Ferro and rode up to the fence to wait for
Lorelei and Aladdin. They both looked beautiful in the
sunlight, streaking across the field of alfalfa, Aladdin's
mane flying in the wind, Lorelei's hair streaming behind
her.

She reined up at the fence. Aladdin stretched his neck
and touched muzzles with Ferro.

"They look as if they're glad to see each other."

"Well, I'm glad to see you, Lorelei. I'm just sorry
there's a fence between us."

"There's a gate farther down," she said, crooking her
neck toward the upper stretch of fencing.

"Do you want me to come onto the Rocking H?"

Her eyes flared wildly.

"No, that might not be a good idea. Not now."

"Why?"

"Oh, John, you don't know how I've missed you. I've wanted so much to talk to you. So much has happened."

"Your father?"

"Oh, him," she said, a sharp edge to her tone. "I'm so disgusted with Daddy. And that woman. Ugh."

"Well, it's his business," Slocum said, but he could see there was more on Lorelei's mind than her father's taking up with Cordelia Granby.

"How do you like Aladdin?" Slocum asked, sensing that it might be time to change the subject.

"I love him," she said. "Riding him is like sitting in a rocking chair."

"That's because he's a trotter. He's got a smooth gait."

"John, something's terribly wrong. My father . . ."

"Look, Lorelei," Slocum said, "if you want to talk about him, fine. But before you do, I want you to know I'm investigating him. I think he's responsible for several murders, including the setup of that Mexican boy they hanged the other day, Luis Delgado."

Lorelei's face drained of color. Her mouth opened. She seemed to be gasping for air. He noticed that her upper lip was quivering and he thought she might have been on the verge of either crying or screaming.

"John, oh John," she said. She moved Aladdin closer to the fence, brought him alongside so that her face was close to Slocum's. "It's that land across the way. Daddy wants to buy it and when Mr. Rankins turned him down for a loan, I thought he would have a fit. Then he met the Granbys and I saw a complete change."

"A complete change? What do you mean?"

"Oh, Daddy was very helpful to Norville and Cordelia.

He showed them the property. He introduced them to Mr. Rankins. And then . . ."

"And then Norville Granby was shot dead."

"Yes. And then someone tried to murder you at the hotel, and then I saw Daddy with Cordelia and I got sick to my stomach. I just knew something was wrong. Terribly wrong."

"What did you think?" Slocum asked, as tears began to well up in Lorelei's eyes.

"I—I thought my father might have had something to do with Norville's death. I mean he took up with—with that woman, Cordelia, right away. The same night her husband was murdered. What was I to think? And now it looks as if Mr. Rankins is going to loan Daddy the money to buy that accursed land."

"You're the second person I've heard tell me that the land is cursed," he said. "Why do you say that?"

"Because it is, that's why. Oh, John, I've been thinking about a lot of things since I last saw you. I thought about men who worked for my daddy and who were arrested, tried and hanged. So many. So many. Too many."

"Did you know that Luis Delgado dug up a strongbox or a trunk on that property?"

"Yes," she said, her tears now streaming down her face. "Daddy brought the trunk home and opened it."

"Was there gold in it?"

"No, but Daddy was very excited. It had papers in it, maps, I think. And I heard him say that he had found the key to the other map. Last night, I heard him and Cordelia talking about it and they were going over the first maps he found, which he's had for a long time and the new ones that were in that old trunk."

"So, now your father knows where the gold is buried."

Lorelei nodded.

"Tomorrow, I think, he and Cordelia are going to finalize the loan at the bank. And right after that, she and my father are going to get married."

"If she lives that long," Slocum said.

"What do you mean?" she gasped.

"It seems to me that your father is an opportunist. He takes advantage of people. Uses them for his own ends."

"That's my daddy," she said. "He's ruined my life and my sister's life."

"You have a sister?" Slocum asked.

"Why, yes. A half sister, really. Didn't you know?"

"No, I thought you were an only child. Your father sure seems to dote on you."

"He was married, for a time, to a Mexican woman. They had a daughter. Then her mother died and my father married again and my mother had me. Pandora and I grew up together. After my mother died, she took care of me like an older sister."

"Pandora? The hangman's wife?"

"Yes. Oh, John, didn't you know?"

Slocum swore under his breath.

Now, some of what he had been straining for in his mind was starting to make sense. He felt as if someone had driven a fist into his gut and knocked all the wind out of his lungs.

Pandora Fernandez was Bill Hardesty's daughter. And all those men hanged—innocent men—were stumbling blocks in the path of Hardesty's search for buried gold. It was monstrous, that's what it was.

Slocum's thoughts were interrupted by the sound of hoofbeats in the distance. They were coming fast.

Lorelei looked up, alarmed.

"Someone's coming," she said.

"That would be the posse from town," Slocum said. "They're after me."

"Why?"

"I just killed a deputy sheriff. Who was trying to kill me."

She hesitated only a moment.

"Then, run, John, run. Get away from here as fast as you can."

Slocum looked at her. Her face was animated. Shadows played over the quivering muscles in her jaw and over her cheeks.

"What is it?" he asked quietly.

"My father. Last night. I heard him tell Cordelia that . . ."

The sound of hoofbeats grew louder.

"That I was going to be killed?" Slocum asked.

Lorelei nodded.

Slocum wheeled Ferro and put the spurs to him. Before he had ridden a hundred yards, he heard the crack of a rifle. A bullet sizzled the air over his head. He turned and saw them, three men wearing out leather, bearing down on him with guns blazing. Out of the corner of his eye, he saw Lorelei galloping away on Aladdin.

Now, he thought, her father will know that she talked to me.

Slocum hunched over as more bullets flew at him, frying the air over his head like murderous hornets.

19

Slocum raced Ferro straight up the creek, crossed it and began zigzagging to avoid being hit by rifle fire. He knew his horse was fresher than those of his pursuers, and he had a plan of escape. He had learned the tactic during the war. When an enemy came at you straight on, you must flank him, either through deception or with speed. Slocum knew he had the speed, and he gradually opened the gap between him and the three men who were chasing him. The rifle fire stopped, but Slocum did not.

He made a wide circle and then doubled back toward the creek. He followed it to its juncture with the Rio Grande. He stopped and let Ferro rest and drink, then he moved on toward Del Rio. He joined the main road and let Ferro mingle his tracks with those of other riders and stock which had passed over it that day. Ferro had begun to sweat, but was in no danger of foundering.

Slocum made another wide circle just so he could check his backtrail. He saw no sign of the small posse that had been chasing him. He rode east, using what cover was available, and widened his circle so that he came up on the opposite end of the Hidalgo settlement.

Outside the town, he saw people gathered in a cemetery. He knew they were attending the burial of Luis Delgado. He slipped past them quietly to show his respect. He didn't see Carmen. By the time he reached the village, the mourners were breaking up and streaming back into Hidalgo. He could see that the women were praying with their rosary beads and the men looked downtrodden and sad, shuffling along on sandals like outcast mendicants.

He rode in, until the buildings shielded him from anyone on the outside of the village. People stopped and stared at him; dogs skulked to get out of his way and sleepy cats lounging in the shade eyed him quickly, then went back to dozing.

"You return," Abeja said as Slocum made for the adobe where he had spent the night. The Indian's eyes scanned the horse's flanks, its withers. "You run the horse hard. He breathes like the storm wind."

"Abeja, I've got three men on my trail. I think it's the sheriff."

Abeja's eyes turned steely. He walked up to Slocum.

"You step down."

"There might be trouble if I stay here again." Slocum sat still in the saddle.

"No, you stay. The sheriff no come here."

"He might."

Abeja shook his head.

"He come, I kill. Good men here. We all watch for starman. He no come here."

"I killed one of his deputies, Abeja."

"Which one?"

"Smith."

"They're all bad men."

"I need a place to stay, but I don't want to bring trouble down on the people here in Hidalgo."

"You stay. I will talk to the men here. They will fight on your side."

"I've got a plan," Slocum said. "But there's a lot of risk. I'll need help. But what I plan to do is dangerous."

"You good man, Slocum. You go after the bad men in Del Rio?"

"Yes. All of them. Right up to the judge, Wyman."

"Um. Mighty dangerous, I think."

"Can you help? Will the young men of Hidalgo be willing to risk their lives? It might not work, any of it."

"The men here, young or old, are mad at Judge Wyman and they want justice. They know the town is bad. The judge, the sheriff, the deputies, and one more, most of all, the hangman."

Slocum wondered how much he should tell Abeja. Probably now was not the time. There were still some details to work out. But he wanted that ring of killers brought to justice before they murdered anyone else.

"If the sheriff and his posse come here looking for me, you call me out, Abeja. They're my responsibility. I don't want you or anyone else here to break the law on my account."

"Hidalgo is not part of Del Rio. He has no authority here."

"That's good to know," Slocum said.

"He will not come here on his own."

"Were you not at the funeral?" Slocum asked.

"Why? Luis Delgado is dead. His spirit is in the clouds, in the sky. There is no one in that coffin."

"But you honor your dead, do you not? Your tribe, I mean."

"My tribe honors our dead every day. But we do not bury our dead in the ground. The old ones did not do this. They give the dead body back to the earth. They pray that the spirit rises to the stars, that bright path in the night sky."

"Good point," Slocum said.

Abeja walked with Slocum as he rode to the adobe where he would spend another night.

"I will put up your fine horse," Abeja said.

"Tomorrow, if there's no trouble with the sheriff tonight, I'd like to meet with the men of the town and lay out my plan," Slocum said, as he swung down out of the saddle.

"I will bring them here," Abeja said.

"Good."

"Do you have hunger? There will be food brought to you, as before."

"I could eat," Slocum said. He had not eaten since breakfast, but his mind was on other matters at the moment.

"Rest. I will talk to the men. We are ready to fight with you as our leader."

Slocum smiled.

"I think you will be the leader, Abeja."

"We will see," he said.

Slocum took his saddlebags, rifle and bedroll into the adobe. The tiredness struck him as soon as he laid out his bedroll. He was surprised to see that someone had put curtains on the window and swept the little house out. It looked very neat and clean, and there was a jar with water in it on the table where he and Abeja had eaten the night before. Inside the jar was a single wildflower, a yellow daisy that brought a brightness to the room.

Carmen, Slocum thought, and he suddenly felt good about coming back to Hidalgo.

Slocum cleaned his pistol, oiled it and reloaded the cylinder with fresh .45 cartridges. He loved the smell of gun oil, but he knew it carried the scent of death with it.

He had killed a man that day and no amount of cleaning could erase the stain of that death from his weapon. Yet, it had been necessary. Smitty and Jones had meant to kill him. They had waited in ambush for him, like the cowards they were. There could be no fair fight with such men. They were backshooters and skulkers, spineless creatures who deserved no mercy. He was pretty sure that Smitty and Jones had been the men who had gone to his hotel room with shotguns meaning to kill him so that he couldn't testify at Delgado's trial. He couldn't prove it, but he didn't have to. Smitty had made his play and lost. Jones would do the same, eventually. It was in his nature.

As for the others involved in the conspiracy, Slocum knew that he had little hard evidence to convict any of them in a court of law. But in the far corners of the West, there was another law. The law of the six-gun and the rope. Men had to answer for their crimes, and if the law wouldn't handle them, then good men must step up and see to it that justice was served.

In Del Rio, he knew he was fighting against the law itself and could expect no mercy himself. He did have proof that the law was corrupt. When Delgado was hanged, despite his innocence, Slocum knew that he was the man who had to step up and mete out justice. Wyman had violated his oath of office, and so, too, the sheriff and his minions. If the hangings were to stop, if injustice was to be stamped out, Slocum knew that he would have to be the one to put a halt to the criminal activity so rampant in Del Rio.

He thought of Lorelei and felt sad for her. She had to know, by now, that her father was a murderer, that he cared nothing for human life if it stood in the way of gaining personal wealth. And what about her half sister, Pandora? How close was Lorelei to her? And was Pandora as guilty as the others? Did she deserve punishment?

Those were questions that Slocum wrestled with as he
napped, waiting for someone to come to the adobe and
bring his supper. He stood outside and smoked a cheroot,
watching the sun go down over the sleepy village. He
went inside and poured himself a drink of whiskey and
was halfway through it when there was a knock on the
door.

"Come in," Slocum said, knowing the door was not
locked.

Carmen entered, carrying a basket that smelled of corn
and flour tortillas, spicy beef and beans. The food was
covered with a cloth. He took the basket from her and set
it on the table. He could see that she had been crying, but
she wore a fresh flower in her hair. She embraced him
and held on for a long time. But she did not cry now.

"John," she said, "I am glad you are here. I spoke to
Abeja and he said he and the men of Hidalgo will help
you."

He stroked her hair. It was like fine silk, as black and
shiny as a crow's wing. She nestled against him and she
wrapped her arms around his waist, holding him even
tighter.

"You didn't come here to talk about Abeja," he said.

"No. I did not know if you would . . . I mean, I am so
bold. And shameless. Yet, I have fear."

"Fear of what?"

"That you will not want me. I feel so alone and my
house is filled with sadness."

"I know," he said.

"We should eat, John."

"We can always eat. It is not food that you need right
now."

"No," she said.

"Should I light the lamp, Carmen? It's getting dark in
here."

"No, do not light it just yet."

"I don't have much of a bed. No fine furniture."

"I will be your bed," she whispered and pulled away so that she could stand on tiptoe and kiss him. She clasped his neck and pulled his head down. She put her lips against his and he felt the warmth shoot through him like liquid fire. She nibbled at his mouth hungrily and he moved over to his pallet and they sank to the floor.

"What will you think of me?" she asked.

"I think you have much to give a man."

"And you? Do you have much to give a woman? A woman who gives herself so willingly?"

"Yes," he husked. "I think I do."

"I think you do, too," she said, and began unlacing the strands of cotton string that held her blouse together in the front. She slipped her blouse over her head and he saw her shadowy breasts, so pert and comely, and the nipples like little pink faces. He touched her there and the nipples hardened like kernels of dried corn, or little acorns.

He leaned down and kissed each nipple and she shivered all over.

"Oh, John," she breathed. *"Te quiero. Te quiero mucho. Te quiero tanto, tanto."*

"I want you, too, Carmen," he said, as her fingers flew to his gun belt. She began to open the buckle, her hunger flowing into him as she kissed his neck, her lips burning his flesh with the hot flame of her wanton desire.

20

The dusk melted away into darkness and the night enclosed Slocum and Carmen as they coupled on the blanketed sleeping mat inside the adobe. Carmen was warm and willing. The two kissed and explored each other with their hands until she opened to him like a flower. He stiff-armed himself on the pallet and slid into her, then let himself down, burying his cock deep into her steaming cunt. She cried out and her fingernails clawed Slocum's back, raking his spine up and down, sending a sharp tingle through his flesh.

"Oh, yes, John," she cooed, "this is what I have been waiting for, ever since I first saw you."

"I, too," he said, sliding his cock in and out of her steaming sheath. "You're a beautiful woman."

She said something in Spanish that was so soft he didn't catch it, but he knew they were words of love or desire, for her body undulated beneath him, impaling him as he stroked her, slow and steady.

"I brought honey," she said.

"You sure did, Carmen."

She laughed and squirmed beneath him, her delight apparent.

"No, I mean with the food."

"That's the last thing on my mind right now, Carmen."

"Yes, yes."

And she rose against him, matching his rhythm with her own, her arms encircling him, her hips cupping him in a separate embrace.

His balls were on fire and he surged against her with powerful thrusts until she clasped him tightly and began to moan. Her moans turned into soft screams and the night soaked them up as if they were spilled droplets of wine. She crooned soft Spanish words in his ear and he understood them. They were raw, sweet words and added to his enjoyment of her.

"You're all woman, Carmen," he sighed, sinking his shaft to the very hilt. She wriggled her bottom and bucked up against him as he plumbed her deepest depths until she was all wet and warm and the folds of her sex were like warm honey against his skin.

"More, more," she said.

Slocum gave her more.

Faster and faster he stroked her until her screams blazed his eardrums like the lashing tongues of a soaring fire. She thrashed beneath him like a woman caught up in madness and he knew she was pouring out her grief and her love all at once, as if she were in the midst of a whirlwind.

He took her to the heights and back down again, then with the sound of slapping bodies filling the room, he exploded his balls when she was at the peak of her own climax. She screamed softly and raked her fingernails down his back and then dug them in as her body thrashed and quivered for several minutes.

"Ah," she breathed. "So sweet. So good, John."

"Yes," he said, and kissed her on the mouth. He rubbed the sweat on her forehead and buried his face in her hair.

He rolled off of her and lay by her side on the bedroll. For several moments there was only the sound of their breathing in the silence of the room. Starlight beamed through the curtains and the cracks between the cloth and the window frames, filling the floor with tiny dancing lights. From somewhere down the street, they could hear the trilling notes of a guitar as fingers picked out the melody of a sad song of love and betrayal in a minor key.

Off in the distance, a coyote yodeled and a dog yapped quick short barks until someone silenced it with a kick or a stick.

"I was in need of you, John," she said. "After the funeral, I felt so alone, so lost."

"I know how you feel," he said.

"Now, I feel alive. I feel as if I can go on living."

"Yes, that is the job of those who are left behind when a loved one dies. They would want that."

"Do you think so?"

Slocum thought about his brother and his parents.

"Yes," he breathed. "That is why we are given the gift of life. To live it, no matter what."

"You are so wise," she said and touched him, her hand kneading the limp flesh of his sex as though it were a piece of dough. He was becoming aroused again.

Carmen sensed it and took her hand away quickly.

"We must eat," she said, "or the food will grow too cold. And the wine from a cellar may get too hot."

He laughed and got up from the pallet. Slocum was hungry. He watched her dress and then he put his clothes on, strapping on his gun belt. He never knew when he would need that pistol again, and he never felt dressed without it.

Over supper, which included cold chicken, Slocum asked Carmen a few questions.

"Did you know that Pandora Fernandez is Bill Hardesty's daughter?"

"Everyone knows that. And everyone knows that Pandora is the real owner of the Rocking H rancho."

"What?"

"It is said, John, that Pandora witnessed something, a murder they say, at the ranch when she was a young woman. She made her father sign the ranch over to her for her silence."

This revelation stunned Slocum. It put a whole different light on the murders, the search for hidden gold, the hangings, everything.

"Did she see her father kill her mother?" Slocum asked.

Carmen shrugged as she nibbled on a small drumstick.

"That is one of the stories. But one wonders why her father did not kill her, if she was a witness."

"Yes, it does look that way. How could a girl get the upper hand against a grown man?"

Carmen drew a deep breath as if to clear her thoughts, as if to summon up a memory. Slocum waited, knowing she had something important to say.

"There has been much talk about that over the years," Carmen said. "Whispers. There was talk of a scandal."

"A scandal?"

"A Mexican woman, who sometimes went to the Hardesty rancho to clean and cook for Mr. Hardesty and his wife, said that there was scandalous behavior. She said that the girl, Pandora, was very close to her father and, one morning, she saw them in bed together and Bill was mounting his daughter."

"Where was Hardesty's wife at the time?"

"She was sick in the bed. There were other times, too, when Clarita—she was the maid—saw the father and Pandora kissing and she said that they did unspeakable things together behind the mother's back."

"And Pandora's mother never found out?"

"Oh, yes, she did find out. Clarita was there and she heard the yelling and the screaming and the daughter, she told her mother, that she was more of a wife to her father than her mother was. And shortly after that, the mother died."

"How did she die?"

"She drowned in her tub," Carmen said. "Mr. Hardesty said it was an accident and everyone believed him. Clarita said that Mr. Hardesty killed his wife, that he held her head under the water until she could not breathe no more."

"But she didn't see this happen?"

"She drew the bath for Mrs. Hardesty, a Mexican woman named Esmeralda Gomez. Then she saw Mr. Hardesty and he was all wet and he changed his clothes. He told the sheriff that he found his wife in the tub and knew she was dead."

"So Hardesty killed his wife," Slocum said. "And did Pandora see this happen?"

"Clarita said she helped her father drown her mother. She was wet, too, and after that, the father and the daughter, they sleep together like marrieds, and only Clarita knew of this. But she told my mother, and my mother told me."

"And what happened to Clarita?" Slocum asked.

"Ah, you ask the good question. Not very long after that, Clarita was found dead between Hidalgo and the Hardesty rancho. They said that she fell from her horse and broke her neck."

"But you don't believe that, do you, Carmen?"

Carmen finished eating and put down her fork. She looked at Slocum, his face half shadowed, half golden from the lamplight.

"No, I think Clarita was murdered. Like so many others."

Slocum pushed his plate away and took a swallow of wine from his glass. His mind was full of grisly pictures, from the war, from battles he had fought since then, and from the images Carmen had conjured for him.

And, finally, he saw in his mind a young girl in her father's lustful clutches, becoming a young woman, all twisted inside from carnal abuse at the hands of Bill Hardesty, a witness, perhaps a participant, in murder, growing up with all those secrets and all that power, taking delight in watching men die, watching men swing at the end of a rope, their necks broken like Clarita's. He saw, finally, a monster and her name was Pandora.

As Slocum thought of these things, a final plan began forming in his mind. Pandora, he believed, was a tormented woman, and so, too, probably, were those who had fed on her hate and lust and given her free rein. She had been allowed to hide behind her husband and her father, and those who knew the truth, turned their heads and looked the other way.

Now was the time to splash light in the shadows, to light a torch that would burn away the darkness and the evil of all those years. Now, he knew, was the time to stop listening to all those rumors and finally proclaim the truth. Now was the time to shed light on the black caverns where all these people dwelled, to drive them out in the open where all could see them for what they were—murderers and cowards with greedy hearts and callous souls.

"What is it, John?" Carmen asked, staring at Slocum. "You are thinking of something, no?"

"Yes," he said, getting up from the table. "I am thinking this has gone on long enough. All the killings, all the hangings, all the lies."

He walked to where his frock coat lay draped over the

back of a chair and dug out a cheroot. He struck a match. His face was grim in the harsh glare of the flame as he lit his cheroot.

Carmen shrank back, as if she had suddenly seen an apparition.

"Tomorrow," Slocum said, "I am going after all of them. One by one."

"What will you do?" she asked. "Kill them?"

"The question is, Carmen, what will they do?"

He walked outside, into the night, drawing smoke through the cheroot, the end of it glowing like an angry eye. He walked out under the stars to work out the final details of his plan.

Carmen did not follow him, but stayed inside the adobe, struck dumb by what she had seen in Slocum's eyes, awed by the power that radiated from him when his jaw hardened and his fists clenched and his shoulders widened with the weight of the determination he carried.

She stayed inside.

And she shuddered, fearful of the horror that she knew would happen.

21

Slocum knew he would never remember all of their names, but he made a point of shaking hands with each of the men Abeja brought to the gathering in Hidalgo. He was impressed with the number of young men who showed up to hear what Slocum had to say.

"You must be a powerful persuader, Abeja," he said.

"They want to help, Slocum. They know what you are doing. Like you, they want justice."

"What I'm doing is not exactly legal," Slocum said.

"What has been done to the people of Hidalgo was not legal."

Slocum looked out over at the assemblage and cleared his throat. Someone had brought a large box for him to stand on so that he could tower above them. He knew it gave him the look of someone in authority, and it was just what he needed.

"Men," he said in Spanish, "thank you for coming here."

There was laugher, followed by resounding applause. Slocum knew they were glad that he was speaking to them in their language. He had learned Spanish over the years and knew that it helped him greatly, especially in a state like Texas.

But he knew he was asking no easy thing. Especially since wherever he went, whether it be Colorado or Missouri or Kansas, the Mexicans he encountered were often loyal to the death for their employers.

"I am going to ask you to do some things for me that will be against the law. But we are against the law that is now in Del Rio. The law there is very bad and I am going to see that justice comes to Del Rio. With your help."

There was more applause.

"Do not applaud," he said. "Just listen. Please."

All of the men nodded soberly. Slocum went on.

"After I speak to you, I will put you in groups. Each group will have a job to do. Now, we will need horses, not only to ride, but two to haul a kind of wagon. Do you have horses?"

Several of the men nodded. One man spoke up, addressing Slocum.

"We do not have many horses, but we know where to steal some."

More laughter. Slocum grinned.

"That's the spirit," he said. "You do not have to steal them, just borrow some until this is over."

The men laughed again and some whooped.

"*Viva* Slocum," one man shouted, and the others took up the chorus, shouting the same cheer.

Slocum held up his hands to stop them from any further demonstration.

"Each of you will need a horse and we need at least two extra to pull that wagon."

"What wagon?" a man asked.

"The gallows wagon," Slocum said and the cheers were deafening.

"*Vamonos*," the men cried. "Let's go."

Again, Slocum held up his hands for silence so that he could continue.

"Do you have weapons? Guns? Rifles? Pistols?"

All of the men nodded and cried out that they did.

Slocum broke the men up into small groups and told each group what he wanted them to do. He made sure that Abeja was with him as he spoke to each group of men. When he was satisfied that they all understood their roles, Slocum waited while those who had horses saddled up or rode bareback.

Some men were sent to "borrow" more horses. These packed double on their horses and carried ropes. Some he sent to the Hardesty ranch to bring Bill and Cordelia into town, telling them to meet Slocum at the courthouse by noon. He warned them not to harm Lorelei, and if possible, to keep her at the ranch by telling her that he was riding out to see her and explain. He hoped that would keep her there, out of harm's way. He wasn't sure how Lorelei would take his kidnapping her father.

He spoke to the men who had the most demanding task. They had appointed a leader recommended by Abeja, one Juan Torres.

"Juan, here is some money. I want one of you, as quietly as you can, to go to the mercantile and buy ten gallons of red paint and six brushes, one for each of you. Then I want you to hook up two horses to the gallows and pull it to a place where you can paint every inch of it red. Get the brightest red paint they have. Do you understand?"

"Yes," Torres said.

"And get me a half dozen of these cheroots," Slocum said, pulling one of the thin cigars from his waistcoat. Torres laughed and snatched the cheroot from Slocum's hand. Slocum lashed out his hand to retrieve it, but Torres held it high in the air behind his head.

"For a sample," he said, grinning.

Slocum laughed and nodded his approval.

Finally, Slocum issued the last of his instructions.

"We will all enter the town like ghosts," he said. "Arriving by ones and by twos so that we do not cause suspicion. Those of you who are leaders will arrange to meet at your appointed places. If we all work together, we will not fail our mission. And that mission is to finally bring justice to the city of Del Rio.

As the men dispersed, Slocum grabbed Abeja's arm.

"I want to say good-bye to Carmen," he said.

"Well, go there," Abeja said. "She is in your little house. She did not return home."

"What?"

Abeja grinned.

"I think she is in love with you, Slocum. There are flowers in her cheeks and a sparkle in her eye."

"How do you know this, and I don't?" Slocum said.

Abeja tapped his head.

"Wisdom comes with age," he said.

Slocum grimaced and walked off to see Carmen.

"Have my horse ready, Abeja."

"It will be done, Master," Abeja chided.

Carmen was inside the adobe. She had cleaned it up and she had brought in a bed, with help, he imagined, to replace the mat on the floor. His bedroll was neatly rolled up and sitting by the door, with his saddlebags and his rifle in its scabbard. The Greener was inside the bedroll, just the way he always packed it himself.

"I came to say good-bye," he said. "Abeja and I, and the others, are going to Del Rio."

"I know. I will be waiting here for you when you return."

"I hope I return."

"You will," she said.

He took her in his arms and she held on to him, squeezing him with her arms.

"*Ten cuidado*," she said. "Be careful."

"I will."

He kissed her, then picked up his gear and walked away. When he turned, she stood in the doorway. She waved at him. He waved back.

Something tugged at his heart as he passed from her view. Carmen was the kind of woman who could grow on a man. But he didn't plan to spend the rest of his life in Del Rio. When he had finished what he wanted to do, he would ride on, as he always did. His life was too dangerous for him to even think about having a permanent woman in it. Still, she would be one to come back to. Someday.

Slocum and Abeja were the last to leave Hidalgo. It was still early in the morning, but the sun had burned the dew off the wildflowers and the sagebrush. Quail were piping and meadowlarks flitted from rock to rock. The lizards had not yet come out to sun themselves and the armadillos had gone to sleep in shady places to await the setting of the sun.

"Where do we go, you and I, Slocum?" Abeja asked when they were some distance from Hidalgo and they could see the whitewashed adobes of Del Rio shining in the sunlight.

"You and I are going to pay a visit to Sheriff Blandings."

"You are going to kill him?"

"Not if he comes along peaceably, Abeja. I want him to perform one last duty in office before I deal with him."

"And, what is that?"

Slocum turned to him and grinned.

"Why Blandings and his deputy, Jones, are going to

walk with us to the courthouse," he said. "And they are going to arrest Judge Wyman."

"You are going to put him in the jail?"

"No, I'm going to have Fernandez hang him. Right in front of the whole damned town."

Abeja grinned.

"*Tu estas loco*," he said. "You are crazy."

"Well," Slocum said, "somebody's got to be."

Abeja broke into laughter and he was still chuckling when they rode up to the sheriff's office.

The door was open. Curtis Blandings was sitting at his desk, playing a game of solitaire with a worn deck of cards. He looked up when Slocum and Abeja walked in. His jaw dropped in surprise.

"Jonesy," Blandings called.

The door to the jail itself opened and Jones appeared, his face lathered with soap, a straight razor in his hand. He wasn't wearing a gun belt.

"Good morning, Sheriff," Slocum said, in a voice bursting with amiability. "Jonesy. Have a seat, son."

"What's your damned business here, Slocum?" Blandings asked, his hands flat on the table, covering the array of cards turned faceup.

"I want you and your deputy, Jones, here, to come with me to the courthouse, Blandings. I'm going to make a citizen's arrest."

"What?"

"You heard me. Now stand up and slip off that gun belt. You won't be needing it."

Jones had sat down, a dumbfounded look on his face. Slocum turned to him.

"Deputy Jones, go with Abeja here and wipe the lather off your face. If you make one funny move, he's going to blow a hole in your belly. Got that?"

Jones started to shake. He stood up.

Abeja aimed his rifle at Jones. He cocked it and the sound made Jones jump. He dropped the razor and it clattered to the floor.

Slocum drew his pistol and pointed its snout at the sheriff. Blandings got up from his chair slowly and started unbuckling his gun belt.

"Just step around your desk, Blandings."

As he did, Slocum leaned over the desk and waved his left arm across it. His hand scattered the cards and swept them from the desk onto the floor.

"You were losing, anyway, Blandings," he said.

Blandings's face drained of color.

"You won't get away with this, Slocum. You're breaking the law. And I still don't know who I'm supposed to arrest."

"You don't? I'm surprised, Blandings. I thought you had enough brains to figure that one out."

"Why, there ain't no criminals over to the courthouse. 'Sides some clerks, there's only the bailiff."

"That would be my good friend, Rufus Early, I believe," Slocum said.

"You want me to arrest Rufus?"

"Oh, yes. He's a guilty man. We might even give him a fair trial."

"Well, if that just don't take the cake. You arrestin' a man of the law. It won't hold up in court."

"Whose court would that be?" Slocum asked.

"Why, Judge Wyman's court, of course."

"Judge Wyman doesn't have a court anymore."

"Huh?" The sheriff cocked his head, a quizzical look on his face.

"He's the other one," Slocum said.

"The other one what?"

"The other man you're going to arrest this morning."

Blandings spluttered, searching for the words that he wanted to spit out.

"Why, you damned fool, Slocum. You're the one who's going to hang over this. You're crazy."

"So I've heard," Slocum said, a wide grin on his face.

Abeja returned with Jones, whose face was now free of froth.

"Gentlemen," Slocum said. "Shall we take a walk over to the courthouse? Blandings, you lead out. I'll be right behind you and I've got an awful itchy finger this morning."

"You son of a bitch," Blandings said.

"Tsk, tsk," Slocum clicked, "let's not bring up family matters right now."

Blandings walked out the door, Slocum right behind him. The sheriff looked like a very sick man.

22

Rufus Early, Slocum thought, took his job entirely too seriously.

When he and Abeja approached the judge's chambers with Blandings and Jones, Early came out from behind his desk like a storm boiling up out of the Gulf of Mexico.

"What the hell's going on here?" Early demanded.

"We're here to arrest the judge," Blandings said, with Slocum's pistol poking him in the back. He choked on the words.

"You all get the hell out of here," Early said. His hand started for his pistol.

"I wouldn't do that if I were you, Rufus," Slocum said.

"You go to hell, Slocum," Early said, completing the move. His hand touched the walnut grips of his Smith and Wesson .38 and his fingers wrapped around the butt. He jerked the revolver from its holster and that was as far as he got.

Slocum stepped to one side, cocked the hammer back on his .45 Colt and squeezed off a shot. The Colt bellowed and spat flame and lead. Early didn't even have time to register a look of surprise on his face as the lead bullet hammered him in the belt buckle, blowing a clean hole through it and the softness of his protruding belly.

Early doubled over. The pistol in his hand dangled from two fingers for a moment like an anvil hanging from a tree root at the edge of a cliff, then thudded on the floor. Blood gushed from Early's abdomen, spilling onto his crotch as he fell to his knees. He looked up at Slocum, his face contorted in pain. His lips were working, his mouth moved, but nothing came out except a curdled gurgle that sounded like a man hawking night phlegm. He toppled over and there was a stench from him as his sphincter muscle relaxed and he voided himself in his trousers.

"God almighty," Jones whined. "You didn't have to go and shoot poor old Rufus now."

"You want to join him, Jonesy?" Slocum said, and stepped back behind Blandings.

Just then, the door to the judge's chambers burst open and a young woman rushed out, a notebook in her hand. She took one look at Early and let out a high-pitched scream that curdled the blood of all within hearing distance.

A moment later, Judge Wyman emerged, robeless, his suit rumpled, his string tie askew, his eyes popped out like a pair of squeezed marbles.

Wyman took in the scene at a glance, and his face puffed out and turned a rosy hue. His neck swelled like a bull in the rut and the veins stood out on his temples like blue worms.

"What in blazing hell is going on out here?" Wyman roared.

"Blandings, arrest the judge. Put his hands behind his back and cuff him," Slocum ordered.

Blandings hesitated.

Wyman glared at Slocum.

"Have you lost your senses, Mr. Slocum?" Wyman said.

"I'm arresting you for murder and conspiracy to commit murder," Slocum said. "In the name of the people of Del Rio."

Slocum prodded Blandings in the back with the muzzle of his pistol. Blandings fiddled with the pair of handcuffs hanging from his belt. They unsnapped and he stepped forward.

"Sorry, Judge Wyman," the sheriff said. "Slocum's got a gun at my back."

Wyman started to turn and go back into his office, fixing Blandings with a sharp look of contempt.

"You take one more step, Wyman," Slocum said, "and you won't have to hang. I'll put your lights out here and now."

Wyman turned savagely and glared at Slocum. He looked down at the body of Early.

"You've already committed murder here, Slocum. That's a hanging offense. You can't get away with this. Even if I declare you insane, which you most probably are, the townsfolk would string you up to the nearest cottonwood tree."

"A lot you know about the townsfolk, Wyman. Blandings, put those handcuffs on the judge or you'll join Early there on the floor."

The judge fumed, but he evidently knew Slocum meant business because he submitted to Blandings, turning around, and putting both hands behind him. The sheriff snapped on the cuffs and locked them.

"Now what?" Blandings asked.

"Back to the jail, for a while," Slocum said.

Slocum and Abeja locked Wyman, Blandings and Jones up in separate cells, then locked the sheriff's office and hung a sign on it that read CLOSED.

Slocum untied Ferro's reins at the hitchrail in front of the sheriff's office. Abeja was already mounted on his burro.

"Follow me," Slocum said, and turned down Main Street.

They then met up with others in Slocum's band of Hidalgans, who had slipped into town and were waiting at various places along the main street. He looked up in the sky and measured the sun's passage across the heavens. He had time; everything had gone fairly smoothly, so far.

"Now, what?" Abeja asked.

"Two of these men can guard the jail, but they don't have to be right out in front. Just tell them to keep an eye out for anyone trying to break out our prisoners."

Abeja picked two men and translated Slocum's orders into Spanish.

"Now, we go see how the painting is coming. The other men here should go to the house of Fernandez and make sure they stay put. Do you know where Pandora and her husband live?"

Abeja nodded. He pointed off to the north.

"Fernandez, he have a big house at the edge of Del Rio on a little creek. He used to live in Hidalgo before he got married, and we know him. But he does not invite us to his grand house anymore."

"You mean not since he married Pandora," Slocum said.

"Not since he got the job as the hangman."

The gallows on wheels stood in the shade a block from Main Street where Slocum's men had taken it. Five men were working furiously on it with brushes.

"Just before noon," Slocum said to Juan Torres, "haul it to the town square."

"The paint will not dry by then," Juan said.

Slocum grinned. "The wetter the better."

"Does it look like the blood?"

"It sure as hell looks like blood," Slocum said.

Slocum and Abeja rode back to the jail. On the way, he was confronted by Vernon Cunningham, who had come rushing out of the newspaper office.

"Mr. Slocum, hold up," Cunningham yelled.

Slocum reined up, as did Abeja.

"What's going on, Slocum? I'm hearing stories that I can't believe!"

"What did you hear?"

"Judge Wyman's secretary came dashing into my office a few minutes ago and said you had shot Bailiff Early and arrested Judge Wyman. She said you had Sheriff Blandings and his deputy, Larry Jones, at gunpoint and that they were following your orders."

"That's not much of a story, Cunningham," Slocum said. "But you be at the town square at noon if you really want a headline."

"What's at the town square?"

"Oh, the usual," Slocum said. "A gallows and a public hanging."

Slocum thought the newspaper publisher was going to have a fit right there on the street.

"Is all this true, then?"

"Yep," Slocum said. "Judge Wyman is cooling his heels in jail and we're about to bring the hangman downtown to put a noose around Judge Wyman's neck. Right out in front of God and everyone."

"Gawdamighty, Slocum, have you gone completely mad?"

"Maybe," Slocum said. "You be the judge. In fact, you may have to be. Wyman won't be sitting in court anymore in Del Rio."

Slocum left Cunningham swearing a blue streak in the middle of the dirt street.

"Go get the sheriff, Abeja," Slocum said, when they reached the jail. "Get the sheriff's pistol, eject all the cartridges and stick it in his holster. I'll go out back and bring his horse out front."

A few minutes later, the three men were riding toward the north edge of town.

"I hope this works," Slocum said, as they neared the arch of the gate leading to the Fernandez house.

"Blandings, this is as far as Abeja and I go. I want you to ride up to the house and knock on the door. Don't go inside. Don't tell Fernandez anything but what I tell you. If you make any false move, I'll drop you with my Winchester. I'll have you in sights the whole way."

"What do you want me to say?"

"I want you to tell Fernandez that Judge Wyman found me guilty and wants me hanged at noon today. Tell him to bring his rope."

"How do I know you won't kill me anyway?"

"Why, you're the sheriff, aren't you, Blandings? You've got to see that there's law and order in Del Rio when this is all over. But don't tempt me. One false move."

Blandings gulped and rode off as Slocum and Abeja took up positions where they could watch, but not be seen.

Slocum saw someone come to the door after Blandings knocked. Carlos Fernandez stepped out onto the porch. A moment later, Blandings turned and left. Fernandez dashed inside the house.

"So far, so good," Slocum muttered to Abeja.

"You have the mind of a devil, John Slocum."

Slocum grinned.

"Before the day is out," he said, "I may grow horns on my head."

Abeja laughed as they waited for Blandings to ride up. Slocum looked up at the sky again.

The only thing missing, so far, was Hardesty and Cordelia Granby. He hoped that by the time he got back into town the rancher and the widow would be right where he wanted them, standing near a bloody gallows, waiting for justice to be served.

23

The gallows stood in the town square, dripping with what looked like blood. People began gathering as word spread that something extraordinary was going to happen. The rumors flew from mouth to ear just the way Slocum had known they would. At the jail, he released Wyman and Jones. Those men from Hidalgo who had been outside, watching the jail, were all in the sheriff's office in obedience to Slocum's orders.

"Strip him," Slocum said, pointing to Judge Wyman. "Just leave him with socks and shorts."

"Who me?" Wyman asked, as Slocum fixed him with a look.

"Yes, you."

"This is an outrage," Wyman said.

"Oh, this isn't the half of it, Wyman." Slocum smiled. "You believe in justice, don't you? Well, you're going to get justice today, all right."

"You bastard," snarled Wyman as Blandings helped him off with his tie. In moments, Wyman stood there, white-skinned, bare except for his feet and privates, looking like a plucked chicken. The Mexicans in the room snickered. Wyman scowled.

"Blandings, there stands your judge," Slocum said. "Defrocked. Now march him to the gallows. Jonesy, you walk with him. We'll all be right behind you."

The procession picked up a crowd as it made its way to the plaza in the center of town. One of the Hidalgo Mexicans led their horses and Abeja's burro behind them. One of those who came up to Slocum as he reached the town square was Emory Davis.

Slocum saw the attorney heading toward them and smiled. For once, Davis seemed to have lost his composure. He was definitely ruffled because he seemed all feet as he stumbled and faltered, dodging those who got in his way.

"Mr. Slocum," Davis said, "tell me that isn't Judge Wyman practically buck naked."

"I can't tell you that, Mr. Davis."

"My God, man, what are you planning to do with him? And how come the sheriff is helping you?"

"The sheriff has had his teeth pulled. There are no bullets in that pistol he's packing. As for the judge, he's going to stand up there on that gallows with a rope around his neck."

Davis's face turned ashen as he walked along beside Slocum. They came up to the gallows and the crowd gasped, as if it had had the wind knocked out of it.

"Stand Wyman around in back of the gallows in the shade. Any sign of the hangman yet?"

"*Ya vienen Fernandez y su esposa*," one of the Mexicans said. "Here comes Fernandez and his wife now."

"Good," Slocum said.

Emory Davis spluttered over the words in his mouth.

"Mr. Slocum, as a member of the court, I must advise you that this is highly illegal. What you're doing is a criminal offense."

"Calm down, Emory," Slocum said. "Judge Wyman

himself is a criminal offense. And he's only part of the necktie party."

"Egads, are you going to hang the whole town?"

"Not a bad idea, but no. Just relax, Davis. Enjoy this moment. It might even be historic."

Slocum stepped up to Blandings.

"You get set, Sheriff. I want Fernandez up on that gallows when I bring Wyman up." He turned to the men from Hidalgo who were all around him, armed to the teeth.

He spoke to them in Spanish.

"Don't shoot Fernandez if he tries to run," he said. "But if he looks like a rabbit, you all aim your guns at him and make sure he knows you might shoot him."

Carlos and Pandora Fernandez rode up, unsuspecting of anything being amiss. He was grinning and his wife was acting the regal lady. They dismounted and tied their horses at a hitchrail in front of a dry goods store. Fernandez united his things in back of the cantle and hefted the canvas sack containing his rope and slung it over his shoulder. He and Pandora walked toward the gallows. Then they both looked up and saw that it was glistening with fresh red paint. They halted. Two of the Hidalgans came up behind them and prodded them with rifles.

"Walk," one of the men said, in English.

"What have they done?" wailed Fernadez.

"Now," Slocum said, prodding the sheriff. "Escort Fernandez up on the gallows platform."

Blandings stepped out and met Fernandez. Pandora shrank back, looked all around, her face a mask. Color had begun to creep up her neck.

"Take your position, Carlos," Blandings said, his voice quavering with fear. He knew the guns were on him.

"Where is the prisoner?" Fernandez croaked.

"I'll bring him up when you get up there."

With the sheriff behind him, Fernandez removed the rope from the sack and lugged it up the steps. As the crowd watched, he secured it to the gallows beam, tested it. He put a foot on the platform and saw that it was secure. He turned to Blandings.

"Who in hell painted this gallows?" he asked. "The paint is still wet and it's all over my boots."

Blandings was at a loss for words.

Slocum grabbed Wyman and shoved him around the side of the gallows. He marched him up the steps.

"I did," Slocum said.

Fernandez dropped his jaw in surprise as Slocum pushed Wyman under the rope.

"What the hell's the meaning of this, Slocum? Judge, didn't I come here to hang Slocum?"

"Put the rope around Wyman's neck, Fernandez," Slocum said.

"I will not."

Slocum drew his pistol. A collective gasp escaped from the crowd, which had now swelled to hundreds.

"If you don't, I'll shoot you where you stand," Slocum said. He thumbed back the hammer and the click could be heard from boardwalk to boardwalk in the plaza.

"Judge, what should I do?" Fernandez said. "I can't hang you."

"If you don't put that rope around Wyman's neck," Slocum said, "it's going to go around yours. Now, do it. Quick."

With fumbling hands, Fernandez moved Wyman into the correct position. He pulled the noose down and slipped it over the judge's head. He hesitated before tightening it. Slocum gestured with his pistol and Fernandez pulled on the knot until the rope was tight around Wyman's neck.

"Now, step aside," Slocum told Fernandez.

Fernandez stepped to one side on a line with the judge. Slocum walked to the front of the platform and looked down at Pandora.

"Bring her up here," he told the two Mexicans who flanked her.

Pandora bolted, started to run. The two men grabbed her and wrestled her to the stairs. They pulled and pushed her up to the platform until she stood next to her husband.

"You bastard," she said to Slocum.

He smiled at her.

"We'll start the proceedings very soon now," Slocum said. The crowd began murmuring among themselves, asking questions, shouting out cheers and jostling among one another for a better look at the strange things that were happening in the very center of their city.

Then, the murmur changed and the crowd parted.

Slocum looked down the street and saw the Hidalgans escorting Bill Hardesty and Cordelia Granby toward him.

"What is this?" Blandings asked.

"A gathering of the guilty," Slocum said, a wry smile on his lips.

Then he looked down at Hardesty, who sat on his horse, a look of rage on his face. Cordelia looked bewildered and scared. Her eyes moved like marbles in a tumbler, her gaze darting all around and up at Slocum.

"Slocum, are you behind this?" Hardesty asked.

"Come and join us up here, Bill," Slocum said. "Cordelia, you can just stay down there and watch. Both of you climb out of the saddle."

Hardesty reined his horse over, trying to turn it but Slocum's guards grabbed him, then moved in to drag Hardesty from the saddle. Others helped Cordelia dismount.

"Bring him up here," Slocum ordered and two men wrestled Hardesty up the steps. He fought them all the way, elbowing and kicking until they released him and stood by for further orders.

The crowd began to get noisier, shouting and clapping.

"What's going on?" someone yelled and others took up the chant. Some people began clapping and others joined in until it sounded like the finish of an outdoor concert.

Slocum holstered his Colt, easing the hammer back down to half-cock. He held up both arms, then brought his hands down in a gesture meant to quiet the crowd. Grumbling and whispering, the crowd slowly grew silent and pushed forward in packed bunches to hear what Slocum was going to say.

"Now, listen carefully," he said. "What's happening here concerns each and every one of you who live and work in Del Rio. My name is John Slocum and I'm here to help you bring justice back to your town."

The crowd cheered and Slocum raised his arms again. They quieted down quickly.

"Slocum, you bastard," Hardesty said, "I demand you stop this farce right now."

Slocum turned and speared Hardesty with a hard look.

"Shut up, Hardesty," he said.

Then, he turned back to the crowd.

"A couple of days ago," Slocum said, "Judge Wyman here sentenced an innocent man to death. The man's name was Luis Delgado. The judge knew he was innocent. So did the bailiff, who is now dead. So did the sheriff and his deputies. And so did Carlos Fernandez, the hangman. More importantly, so did Pandora Fernandez, his wife, who is standing up here on this bloody gallows. And so did Bill Hardesty, Pandora's father."

The crowd gasped so loudly it was as if a brisk wind had sprung up from nowhere and riffled through the town.

"An innocent man died because of the greed of Bill

Hardesty and his daughter Pandora," Slocum continued. "And Luis Delgado was not the first to die on these gallows because of the people you see here. Innocent men have been hanged here because of Hardesty's greed and the heartlessness of all who are standing behind me. If you want proof, read this week's newspaper, because Mr. Cunningham is going to publish the evidence. He is going to name names, both of the victims and of their murderers."

Another collective gasp from the crowd filled the air with a whooshing sound.

"Now, I can take the law into my own hands," Slocum went on. "In fact, I already have. I can hang Judge Wyman right here and now. But I won't be the judge and the jury. You citizens of Del Rio will be that judge and jury. So, make your decision. Do you want to hang Judge Wyman and all those up here who are guilty of several murders, or do you want to bring law and order back to Del Rio? You'll have to elect a new judge. You'll have to try these people in a new court of law and you'll have to abide by the court's decision."

"Hang 'em all," a man in the crowd shouted.

Some others took up the chant, but others in the assemblage quieted them down.

"Listen to Slocum," someone else cried out.

"There is blood on these gallows," Slocum said. "Innocent blood. That's not red paint you see, but blood, human blood, and these people are responsible for every drop of it. But I say that you must choose between law and lawlessness. If you hang these people, you will be breaking the law. But if you jail them and get a new judge and try them legally, you will have triumphed over evil. You will have brought justice back to Del Rio."

The crowd went silent.

Slocum looked down the street and saw a rider coming

at a gallop. He recognized her, her hair flying in the wind, her beautiful form part of the white horse she rode, Aladdin.

It was Lorelei Hardesty.

Slocum stepped back, waiting for the crowd's response.

"Justice," a woman shouted.

"Justice, justice, justice," the crowd chanted.

"Jail them."

"Kill them."

Slocum smiled.

"Raise your hands if you want to follow the law with these people," he shouted.

Nearly everyone in the crowd raised a hand.

"So be it," Slocum said. "You have chosen law and you will achieve justice."

The crowd erupted in a roar of approval. Men crowded around the gallows and some rushed up to the platform and began grabbing Fernandez, Pandora, Hardesty and the sheriff. Slocum removed the noose from around Wyman's neck and men snatched him away, hurled him down the steps. He landed in an ignominious heap at the bottom of the stairs.

Slocum walked down the steps, the last to go, and he stood in front of Lorelei, who sat atop Aladdin.

"I don't know what went on here," she said, "but it appears you've won."

"I'm sorry about your father," he said.

"Don't be, John. I knew why the men came and took him away. I've known for a long time. I just didn't want to admit it. I didn't want to think of my father as a murderer. But he is."

"And you'll accept whatever punishment he gets in a court of law?"

"I will. Oh, I'll cry and I'll have regrets and I'll feel guilty."

"I can tell you a way to get over it," he said.

She slid from the saddle and melted into Slocum's arms.

"Tell me," she said.

"Just think about Luis Delgado and all the others your father had murdered on the gallows. Just think about them and how their lives were cut short."

"I will," she said, stepping back and standing on tiptoes to kiss Slocum. "And I'll think about you, too, John Slocum."

They embraced as the crowd surged around them and melted away. Slocum looked over at Cordelia who was flanked by Torres and Abeja. He nodded, and they grabbed her arms and started walking her toward the jail.

Lorelei began to cry and Slocum wondered whether it was for her father or because she was happy to be free of the heavy load she had carried for so long.

Perhaps, he thought, he would never know.

Watch for

SLOCUM AND THE CROOKED SHERIFF

309th novel
in the exciting SLOCUM
series from Jove

Coming in November!

JAKE LOGAN
TODAY'S HOTTEST ACTION WESTERN!

Explore the exciting Old West with one of the men who made it wild!

J. R. ROBERTS

THE GUNSMITH